"Oh, my goodness. We could have been discovered." Zabrina was breathing in horror. **"Anyone could have walked in at any time."**

Roman shook his head. He had been wondering how he could tell her what she needed to know. He just hadn't been sure how to go about it. But now he was. There was a perfectly simple way of alerting her to the simple fact that was going to change her fate forever. His, too. Yet wasn't there a part of him that felt a kind of *relief* at the prospect that he would no longer need to marry her? No longer need to marry *anyone*.

"Nobody would have walked in," he declared with icy certainty.

She gave a nervous laugh. "You can't possibly know that."

"Yes, I can."

"How?"

He looked into her forest green eyes and sucked in a deep breath.

"Because my name is not Constantin Izvor and I am not the chief bodyguard to the royal household. I am—"

"You are the king," she interrupted suddenly, her face growing as white as a summer cloud. "You are King Roman of Petrogoria."

Sharon Kendrick once won a national writing competition by describing her ideal date: being flown to an exotic island by a gorgeous and powerful man. Little did she realize that she'd just wandered into her dream job! Today she writes for Harlequin, and her books feature often stubborn but always to-die-for heroes and the women who bring them to their knees. She believes that the best books are those you never want to end. Just like life...

Books by Sharon Kendrick

Harlequin Presents

Cinderella in the Sicilian's World
The Sheikh's Royal Announcement
Cinderella's Christmas Secret

Conveniently Wed!

His Contract Christmas Bride

The Legendary Argentinian Billionaires

Bought Bride for the Argentinian
The Argentinian's Baby of Scandal

Visit the Author Profile page
at Harlequin.com for more titles.

Sharon Kendrick

ONE NIGHT BEFORE THE ROYAL WEDDING

HARLEQUIN
PRESENTS

Recycling programs
for this product may
not exist in your area.

ISBN-13: 978-1-335-40391-9

One Night Before the Royal Wedding

Harlequin Enterprises ULC
22 Adelaide St. West, 40th Floor
Toronto, Ontario M5H 4E3, Canada
www.Harlequin.com

Printed in U.S.A.

ONE NIGHT BEFORE
THE ROYAL WEDDING

For the gorgeous Pete Crone—with thanks for his help and inspiration, particularly in regard to the Marengo Forest.

CHAPTER ONE

WHO *WAS* SHE?

A puppet, that was who.

Zabrina pulled a face, barely recognising the person she saw reflected back at her. Because the woman in the mirror was an imposter, her usual tomboy self replaced by a stranger wearing unaccustomed silks and finery which swamped her tiny frame. Another wave of panic swept over her. The clock was slowly ticking down towards her wedding and she had no way of stopping it.

'Please don't scowl,' said her mother automatically. 'How many times do I have to tell you? It is not becoming of a princess.'

But at that precise moment Zabrina didn't *feel* like a princess. She felt like an object, not a being. An object who was being treated with all the regard you might show towards a sack of rice being dragged by a donkey and cart towards the marketplace.

Yet wasn't that the story of her life?

Expendable and disposable.

As the oldest child, and a female, she had always been expected to safeguard her family's future, with her hand in marriage offered up to a future king when she was little more than a baby. She alone would be the one able to save the nation from her weak father's mismanagement—that was what she had always been told and she had always accepted it. But now the moment was drawing near and her stomach was tying itself up in knots at the thought of what lay ahead. She turned to face her mother, her expression one of appeal, as if even at this late stage she might be granted some sort of reprieve.

'Please, Mama,' she said in a low voice. 'Don't make me marry him.'

Her mother's smile failed to hide her resolve. 'You know that such a request is impossible, Zabrina—just as you have always known that this is your destiny.'

'But this is supposed to be the twenty-first century! I thought women were supposed to be free?'

'Freedom is a word which has no place in a life such as yours,' protested her mother. 'It is the price you pay for your position in life. You are a princess and the rules which govern royals are different from those of ordinary citizens—a fact which you seem determined to ignore. How many times have you been told that you can't just behave as you wish to behave? These early-morning missions of yours are really going to have to stop, Zabrina. Yes, really. Do you think we aren't aware of them?'

Zabrina stared down at her gleaming silver shoes

and tried to compose herself. She'd been in trouble again for sneaking out and travelling to a refuge just outside the city, fired by a determination to use her royal privilege to actually *do* something to help improve the plight of some of the women in her country. Poverty-stricken women, some under the control of cruel men. Her paltry personal savings had almost been eaten away because she had ploughed them into a scheme she really believed in. She repressed a bitter smile. And all the while she was doing that, she was being sold off to the king of a neighbouring country—in her own way just as helpless and as vulnerable as the women she was trying to help. Oh, the irony!

She looked up. 'Well, I'm not going to be able to behave as I please when I marry the King, more's the pity!'

'I don't know why you're objecting so much.' Her mother gave her a speculative look. 'For there are many other positive aspects to this union, other than financial.'

'Like what?'

'Like the fact that King Roman of Petrogoria is one of the most influential and powerful men in the world and—'

'He's got a beard!' Zabrina hissed. 'And I *hate* beards!'

'It has never prevented him from having a legion of admirers among the opposite sex, as far as I can understand.' Her mother's eyes flashed. 'And you will soon get used to it—for many, a beard is a sign of virility and fertility. So accept your fate with open arms and it will reward you well.'

Zabrina bit her lip. 'If only I could be allowed to take one of my own servants with me, at least that might make it feel a bit more like home.'

'You know that can't happen,' said her mother firmly. 'Tradition dictates you must go to your new husband without any trappings from your old life. But it is nothing more than a symbolic gesture. Your father and I shall arrive in Petrogoria with your brother and sisters for the wedding.'

'Which is weeks away!'

'Giving you ample opportunity to settle into your palace home and to prepare for your new role as Queen of Petrogoria. After that, if you still wish to send for some of your own staff, I am certain your new husband will not object.'

'But what if he's a tyrant?' Zabrina whispered. 'Who will disagree with me for the sake of disagreement?'

'Then you will work with those disagreements and adapt your behaviour accordingly. You must remember that Roman is King and he will make all the decisions within your marriage. Your place as his queen is to accept that.' Her mother frowned. 'Didn't you read those marriage manuals I gave you?'

'They were a useful cure for my recent insomnia.'

'Zabrina!'

'No, I read them,' admitted Zabrina a little sulkily. 'Or rather, I tried. They must have been written about a hundred years ago.'

'We can learn much from the past,' replied her mother serenely. 'Now smile, and then let's go. The train will already be waiting at the station to take you to your new home.'

Zabrina sighed. It felt like a trap because it *was* a trap—one from which it seemed there was no escape. Never had she felt so at the mercy of her royal destiny. She'd never been particularly keen to marry anyone, but she was far from ready to marry a man *she'd never even met*.

Yet she had been complicit in accepting her fate, mainly because it had always been expected of her. She'd been all too aware of the financial problems in her own country and the fact that she had the ability to put that right. Maybe because she was the oldest child and she loved her younger brother and sisters, she had convinced herself she could do it. After all, she wouldn't be the only princess in the history of the world to endure an arranged marriage!

So she had carefully learnt her lessons in Petrogorian history and become fluent in its lilting language. She studied the geography of the country which was to be her new home, especially the vast swathe of disputed land—the Marengo Forest—which bordered her own and would pass into the ownership of her new husband after their marriage, in exchange for an eye-watering amount of cash. But all those careful studies now felt unconnected with her real life—

almost as if she'd been operating in a dream world which had no connection with reality.

And suddenly she had woken up.

Her long gown swished against the polished marble as she followed her mother down the grand palace staircase which descended into an enormous entrance hall, where countless servants began to bow as soon as the two women appeared. Her two sisters came rushing over, a look of disbelief on both their faces.

'Zabrina, is that really you?' breathed Daria.

'Why, it doesn't really look like you at all!' exclaimed little Eva.

Zabrina bit down hard on her lip as she hugged them goodbye, picking up seven-year-old Eva and giving her an extra big hug, for her little sister sometimes felt like a daughter to her. She wanted to cry. To tell them how much she was going to miss them. But that wouldn't be either fair, or wise. She had to be grown-up and mature and concentrate on her new role as Queen, not give in to indulgent emotion.

'I don't know why you don't wear that sort of thing more often,' said Daria as she gazed at the floaty long gown. 'It looks so well on you.'

'Probably because it's not really appropriate clothing for being on the back of a horse,' replied Zabrina wryly. 'Or for running around the palace grounds.'

She hardly ever wore a dress. Even when she was forced into one for some dull state occasion, she wouldn't have dreamed of wearing one like this, with all its heavy embellishments which made it feel as constricting as a suit of armour. The heavy flow of material impeded her naturally athletic movements and she hated the way the embroidered bodice clung to her breasts and emphasised them, when she preferred being strapped securely into a practical sports bra. She liked being wild and free. She liked throwing on a pair of jodhpurs and a loose shirt and jumping onto the back of a horse—and the more temperamental, the better. She liked her long hair tied back out of the way in a simple ponytail, not gathered up into an elaborate style of intricate curls and studded with pearls by her mother's stylist.

Her father was standing there and Zabrina automatically sank to the ground, reluctantly conceding that perhaps it was easier to curtsey in a dress, rather than in a pair of jodhpurs.

'How much better it is to see you look like a young woman for a change,' the King said, his rasping voice the result of too many late-night glasses of whisky. 'Rather than like one of the grooms from the stables. I think being Queen of Petrogoria will suit you very well.'

For one brief moment Zabrina wondered how he would react if she told him she couldn't go through with it. But even if her country *didn't* have an outstanding national debt, there was no way the King would offend his nearest neighbour and ally by announcing that the long-awaited wedding would not take place. Imagine the shattered egos and political fallout which would result if he did!

'I hope so, Papa—I really do,' she answered as she turned towards her brother, Alexandru. She could read the troubled expression in his eyes, as if silently acknowledging her status as sacrificial lamb, but despite his obvious reservations what could the young prince possibly do to help her? Nothing. He was barely seventeen years old. A child, really. And she was doing it for him, she reminded herself. Making Albastase great again—even though she suspected that Alexandru had no real desire to be King.

Zabrina walked through the gilded arch towards the car which was parked in the palace courtyard and, climbing into the back of the vintage Rolls-Royce, she envisaged the journey which lay ahead of her. She would be driven to the railway station where King Roman of Petrogoria's royal train was waiting, with his high-powered security team ready to accompany her. On this beautiful spring afternoon, the train would travel in style through the beautiful countryside and the vast and spectacular Marengo Forest, which divided the two countries. By tomorrow, they would be pulling into Petrogoria's capital city of Rosumunte, where she would meet her future husband for the first time, which was a pretty scary thought. It had been drummed into her that she must be sure to project an expression of gentle gratitude when the powerful monarch greeted her, and to curtsey as deeply as possible. She must keep her eyes downcast and only respond when spoken to. Later that night there would be fireworks and feasting as the first of the pre-wedding celebrations took place.

And two strangers would be expected to spend the rest of their lives together.

Zabrina shot a wistful glance across the courtyard in the direction of the stable block and thought about her beloved horse, which she had ridden at dawn that very morning. How long would it take for Midas to miss her? Would he realise that until she was allowed to send for him one of the palace grooms would take him out for his daily exercise instead of her?

She thought about the bearded King and now her cause for concern was much more worrying. What if she found him physically repulsive? What if her flesh recoiled if—presumably when—he laid a finger on her? Despite her jokey remarks, she had read the book gifted to her by her mother, but she had received most of her sexual education from the Internet and an online version of the Kama Sutra. Even some of the lighter films she'd seen didn't leave a lot to the imagination and Zabrina had watched them diligently, fascinated and repelled in equal measure. She had broken out in a cold sweat at the thought of actually *replicating* some of the things the actors on the screens had been doing. Could she really endure the bearded King's unwanted caresses for the rest of her life?

She swallowed.

Especially as she was a total innocent.

A feeling of resignation washed over her. Of course she was. She'd never even been touched by a man, let alone kissed by one, for her virginity played a pivotal role in this arranged marriage. She thought about another of the books she'd ploughed her way through. The one about managing expectations within relationships and living in the real world, rather than in the fantasy version peddled by books and films. It had been a very sobering read but a rather useful one, and it had taught her a lot. Because once you abandoned all those stupid high-flown ideas of love and romance, you freed yourself from the inevitability of disappointment.

The powerful car pulled away to the sound of clapping and cheering from the assembled line of servants, but Zabrina's heart was heavy as she began her journey towards unwanted destiny.

CHAPTER TWO

'SIR, I URGE you not to go ahead with this madcap scheme.'

Roman's eyes narrowed as he surveyed the worried face of the equerry standing before him, who was practically wringing his hands in concern as they waited in the forecourt of the vast railway station for the Princess to arrive. He wasn't used to opposition and, as King, he rarely encountered any. But then, usually he was the soul of discretion. Of sense. Of reason and of duty.

His mouth hardened.

Just not today.

Today he was listening to the doubts which had been proliferating inside his head for weeks now—doubts which perhaps he should have listened to sooner, if he hadn't been so damned busy with the affairs of state which always demanded so much of his time.

'And what exactly are your objections?' he countered coolly.

Andrei took a deep breath, as if summoning up the courage he needed to confront his ruler. 'Your Majesty, to disguise yourself in this way is a grave security risk.'

Roman raised his brows. 'But surely the royal train will be packed with armed guards who are prepared to give their lives for me, if necessary.'

'Well, yes.'

'So what exactly is your problem, Andrei? Where is the risk in that?'

Andrei cleared his throat and seemed to choose his next words carefully. 'Will the future Queen not be angry to discover that the man she is marrying is masquerading as a commoner and a bodyguard?'

'Why don't you let me be the judge of that?' remonstrated Roman icily. 'For surely the moods of the future Queen are no business of yours.'

His equerry inclined his head. 'No, no, of course not. Forgive me for my presumption. Your wishes, as always, reign supreme, my liege. But, as your most senior aide, I would not be doing my job properly if I failed to point out the possible pitfalls which—'

'Yes, yes, spare me the lecture,' interrupted Roman impatiently as they made their way towards the red carpet where the Petrogorian train was sitting on the platform in all its gleaming and polished splendour of ebony and gold. 'Just reassure me that my wishes have been understood. Are all the other guards up to speed about what they are to do?'

'Indeed they are, my liege. They have been fully

briefed.' Andrei cleared his throat. 'For the duration of the train journey from here to Petrogoria, you have taken on the role of chief bodyguard. A role to which you are well suited, with your expertise in the martial arts as well as your undoubted survival skills.'

'Are you trying to flatter me, Andrei?' enquired Roman drily.

'Not at all, sir. I am simply stating the facts—which are that you are perfectly qualified to act as a bodyguard, for your strength and your sword skills are legendary. And that hitherto you will be known as Constantin Izvor and none of the staff will address you as sire, or Your Majesty. They have also been instructed that under no circumstances are they to bow in your presence or give any clue as to your true, royal identity.'

'Good.'

'And they also know that, along with a female servant, you will have sole access to the Princess.'

'Correct.'

'If I may be so bold, it is also a little strange, sire, to see you clean-shaven.'

Roman's lips curved into a smile, for this was a sentiment he shared with his equerry. He had worn a beard since he was nineteen years old and the thick black growth had always defined him, as had his thick black hair. Even when he had ascended to the throne four years ago, he had not conformed by cutting off the luxuriant mane whose ebony waves had brushed against his collar. The press often commented that it made him look like a buccaneer and sometimes referred to him as the conquering King, and he was not averse to such a nickname. But he had been taken aback by how dramatically a shave and a haircut had changed his appearance and when he'd looked in the mirror, he had been a little startled. He had noticed, too, that many of the palace servants had passed him by without recognising him!

And hadn't that sensation filled him with a sudden sense of yearning and sparked off this brainwave of an idea? He'd realised that this was his first ever taste of anonymity—and that, although it was sweet in the extreme, it was poignant, too. Like being given a glimpse of something very beautiful and knowing you would never see it again. Oh, he had travelled incognito before, especially if he was visiting one of his former mistresses in Europe, but he'd never pretended to be anyone other than a king before, and the sense of occupying the skin of a commoner was curiously liberating.

As he awaited Zabrina's arrival, Roman could sense his aide's surprise showing little sign of evaporating and maybe that was understandable, because he was aware he was behaving in a highly uncharacteristic way. For years he had thought nothing of his long-arranged marriage, for such unions were traditional in royal circles, such as his own. In fact, the only time the convention had been broken had been by his own father, and the disastrous results had reverberated down through the years. It was a mistake he was determined never to replicate, for his parents' short-lived marriage had been enough to sour Roman's appetite for anything defined by the word 'love'.

His mouth twisted. Only fools or dreamers believed in love.

He knew he must wed if he wished to continue the noble line of Petrogoria and it was sensible to select a wife who would fit seamlessly into her role as his queen. Just as he knew that the odds were better if his intended bride was also of royal blood—and this marriage had been brokered many years ago. He would acquire the hugely significant Marengo Forest, and Zabrina's homeland would be bankrolled in exchange. It was a deal designed to satisfy the needs of both their countries and, on paper, it had seemed the perfect pairing. In fact, for many years it hadn't even impacted on his personal life, for he had enjoyed brief relationships with carefully selected women who were chosen for their discretion as much as their shining beauty. His arranged marriage had just been something which was there in the background—like a string quartet playing quietly during a state banquet.

Yet lately, the thought of his impending nuptials to someone who supposedly ticked all the right boxes had started to give him cause for disquiet. A wedding which had always seemed an impossibly long way ahead seemed to have arrived with indecent speed. He had started wondering what kind of woman Princess Zabrina really was and the rumours which had reached his ears about her offered him no reassurance. It was said she was a little too fond of her own opinion, and at times could be feisty. It was also said that she was a rule-breaker and there were claims that she sometimes disappeared and nobody knew where she was. And mightn't that create a problem going forward? Because what if the virgin princess proved to be an unsuitable candidate to sit by his side and help rule his beloved country, and raise his children?

He swallowed and his throat suddenly felt as raw as if it had been lined with barbed wire.

What if she was like his own feckless mother?

A bitter darkness invaded his heart but instantly Roman quashed the feeling. Instead he concentrated on the rather faded gleam of the Princess's Rolls-Royce as it made its stately approach onto the station forecourt, its Albastasian flag fluttering in the light breeze. Soon he would no longer have to rely on conjecture and he would discover what kind of woman Zabrina *really* was. Beginning with her appearance—which up until now he had only ever seen in pictures in which she often appeared to be glaring suspiciously at the lens, as if she didn't like having her photo taken.

And there she was. The car door was opened and a woman stepped out, the tip of her silver shoe contrasting vividly against the scarlet carpet which streamed in front of her like a rush of blood. She moved rather awkwardly in her silken gown as if she was uncomfortable within its rich folds, and Roman felt a sudden unexpected rush of adrenalin as he surveyed her in the flesh. Because she was...

He felt the inexplicable thunder of his heart.

She certainly wasn't what he'd expected. Small of stature and very slim, she looked much *younger* than he'd imagined, although he knew for a fact that she was twenty-three—a decade less than himself. But right now she looked little more than a girl. A girl with the cares of the world on her shoulders if her sombre expression was anything to go by, for there were lines of worry around her full lips. Her smile seemed almost *forced* as he began to walk towards her, though surely that could not be so, since she must have been aware that there were countless women who would have wished to be in her situation.

Who would *not* want to marry the King of Petrogoria?

As he grew closer he could see that her skin was glowing—unusually so—and his eyes narrowed. This wasn't the protected flesh of a pampered princess who spent most of her time beneath gilded palace ceilings. In fact, she had the high colour of someone who was far more comfortable being outside. He frowned, because didn't that feed into some of the gossip he'd heard about her? Yet he noticed that her eyes were an unusual shade of deepest green—as dark as the tall trees of the Marengo Forest, which would soon be his—and that they widened as he

came to a halt in front of her. They were beautiful eyes, he realised suddenly. Rich and compelling,
with a flicker of innocence in their depths. Quell-
ing the brief stab of his conscience at what he was
about to do—because surely one day they would
laugh together about this—he executed a deep bow
and stepped forward.

'Good morning, Your Royal Highness,' he said.
Only now he wished he weren't masquerading as
anyone—because wouldn't his kingly status have
given him licence to lift her hand and press those
tanned fingers to his lips? To inhale the sweet scent
of her skin and acquaint himself with her own dis-
tinctive perfume? He cleared his throat, struck by
the sudden quickening of his blood. 'My name is
Constantin Izvor and I am the chief bodyguard who
will be in charge of your safe passage to Petrogoria.'

'Good morning.'

Zabrina's response was steady but inside she felt
anything *but* steady. She inclined her head in greeting, mainly to hide her face, aware of a disconcerting cocktail of emotions flooding through her which
she didn't want the King's servant to see. Her initial
thought was that the chief bodyguard seemed a little *too* confident and full of himself and her second
was that he was…

She swallowed.

The second was that he was *utterly gorgeous*.

Her heart missed a beat. He was beautiful, there
was no other way to describe him. And he was pow-

erful. Strong. The most incredible-looking man she'd ever laid eyes on. Not that she had a lot of experience in that department, of course, but she'd certainly never seen anyone like him among the dignitaries at official functions, or the palace servants she'd grown up with.

She tried not to stare but it was difficult, because he was better looking than any Hollywood heart-throb and all she wanted to do was to drink him in with her hungry gaze. Zabrina had been taught from birth never to maintain eye contact with anyone— especially not servants—but suddenly that seemed an impossible task. And, since she was surely per-mitted a closer look at the man who had been charged with her protection, she continued with her rapid as-sessment.

Night-black hair was cropped close to his head and his skin gleamed, like softly buffed gold. His features were chiselled and exquisitely sculpted— the faint scar on his jaw the only thing which marred their even perfection. A silky cream shirt hinted at the hard torso beneath and close-fitting trousers were tucked into soft leather boots, emphasising every sinew of his muscular thighs and making the most of his sturdy legs. She could see a sword tucked into a leather belt—and, in his other pocket, the unmis-takable outline of a handgun. These two weapons made him look invulnerable. They made her think of danger. So why was that filling her with a wild kind of excitement, rather than a natural wariness, which surely would have served her better?

Remembering her instructions, she forced herself to look down again—as if it were imperative to study the nervous fingertips which were brushing fretfully over her silky gown. But his image remained stubbornly burned into her memory. She wished her heart rate would steady and that his proximity weren't sending her senses so haywire. Senses which until now she hadn't known she possessed. She felt raw. Vulnerable. Her body felt as if a deep layer of skin had ripped away from it, leaving her almost...*naked*.

Yet as she lifted her gaze upwards once more, it was the bodyguard's eyes which unsettled her most—because they were not so easy to look at as the rest of him. They were hard and cold. The coldest eyes she'd ever seen. Steely-grey, they cut through her like the sword which hung from his belt and were fringed by liquorice-dark lashes which made his gaze appear piercing and...brooding. Suddenly it was impossible to keep a flush of self-awareness from flooding her cheeks, making her shift from side to side in her silver shoes, wondering what on earth was happening to her.

Because she wasn't the type of person to be blindsided like this. The only time she could remember having had a crush on someone—and an innocent one at that—had been for her fencing tutor when she'd been just seventeen. Somebody must have noticed her clumsy blushes whenever he was around because the man had been summarily removed from his employment without her even having had the chance to say goodbye to him. Zabrina remembered feeling vaguely sad—a feeling which had been superseded by indignation that her life should be so rigidly controlled by those around her.

But what she was experiencing now was the very opposite of *innocent*. There was a distracting tightening of her breasts and the pulsing of something honeyed and sweet at the base of her stomach. A faint film of perspiration broke out on her forehead and she thought how horrified her mother would be to see her princess daughter sweating like a labourer.

'Is there anything Her Royal Highness desires before we set off?' Constantin Izvor was saying.

And sudden Zabrina was angry at the nature of her jumbled thoughts. Angry at the way her stomach was fluttering with butterflies. With an effort she composed herself, drawing her shoulders back, and determined to inject a suitable note of command into her voice. 'There is nothing I desire, thank you, Izvor. And since I see no reason for further delay, I suggest we get going. We have a long journey ahead of us,' she said crisply, perfectly aware that her observation was actually an order and hoping her brusque words would shatter the debilitating sense of torpor which had suddenly enveloped her.

The bodyguard looked slightly surprised—as if he wasn't used to being spoken to like that—which alerted Zabrina to a couple of possibilities. Was his employer, the King, especially tolerant with his staff? she wondered. Was Izvor one of those tiresome servants who seemed to think that the trappings of royalty were theirs, too—simply by association? Well, he would quickly learn that he needed to keep his distance from *her*!

'Certainly, Your Royal Highness,' he drawled. 'The train is ready to leave. You have only to say the word and I will ensure we are quickly under way, for I am your most obedient servant.'

Something about his words didn't quite ring true and the hint of a smile playing at the edges of his lips made Zabrina feel as if he were actually *mocking* her, but surely he wouldn't dare do that? Anyway, why was she even giving him a moment's thought, when Constantin Izvor was nothing more than one of the many cogs who kept the royal machine smoothly rolling along?

'Good. Consider the word given. Let's go!' With a quick nod, she began to walk down the red carpet and as the brass band began to play the Albastasian national anthem, Zabrina was surprised by the powerful wave of homesickness which swept over her. From now on she was going to have to listen to the Petrogorian version and, although she had learnt the words by heart, it was not nearly so tuneful.

Constantin Izvor leapt onto the train in front of her, but she refused the helping hand he extended, with a firm shake of her head. Admittedly, it was a very big and old-fashioned train, but she was perfectly capable of negotiating her way up the cumbersome steps into the front carriage without any assistance from the dashing bodyguard. Why, she had spent her life leaping onto the backs of horses which made most people quake!

Yet the thought of him touching her filled her with a disconcerting burst of something which felt like excitement. Why could she suddenly imagine all too vividly how it might feel if those strong fingers tightened around her much smaller hand with a firm grip?

Slightly hampered by the abundant folds of her dress, Zabrina hauled herself up onto the train where a young woman was standing, waiting to greet her. With her blonde hair cut into a neat bob and wearing a simple blue shift dress, she looked more like a member of an airline cabin crew than a royal Petrogorian servant. Constantin Izvor introduced her as Silviana and Zabrina smiled, unable to miss the bodyguard's flicker of surprise when she replied in fluent Petrogorian.

'You speak my language well,' he observed, on a deep and thoughtful note.

'When I am seeking your approval, I will be sure to ask for it!' Zabrina answered coolly and for some reason Silviana winced, as if she had said something untoward.

'I will be sure to remember that in future, Your Royal Highness,' the bodyguard replied gravely. 'And in the meantime, I will escort you to your salon.'

She followed him along the narrow corridor until he threw open a door which led onto a lavishly appointed salon. Zabrina nodded and walked inside but, annoyingly, the bodyguard showed no sign of leaving. He was still standing on the threshold, his steely eyes gleaming, as if he had some God-given *right* to dominate her space and disturb her equilibrium. Zabrina wondered if she should formally dismiss him—yet the stupid thing was that, despite his presumption and his undoubted arrogance, she was strangely unwilling to see him go. It would be like closing the night-time shutters on a spectacular moon—you wouldn't be sure when you'd see all that beauty again.

'How long do you anticipate we'll be travelling for?' she questioned.

He shrugged, a movement which served only to illuminate the powerful ripple of his shoulders beneath his silky shirt.

'Fourteen hours at most, for the train will halt its journey midway, to allow Her Royal Highness a peaceful night of sleep,' he replied smoothly. 'We should reach the capital of Rosumunte before the sun is too high, where the people are already gathering to greet you.'

'Good,' she said, though the word didn't register her sudden rush of nerves at the thought of crowds of people waiting to see her. Would they like her? Would they consider her worthy to be the wife of their King?

'I trust you'll find everything to your satisfaction,' he said.

Zabrina forced herself to look around, trying to take in her surroundings and act as if she cared about them when all she could think about was him. She tried to acknowledge the splendid decoration. The walls were hung with pale lemon silk and several stunning oil landscapes, which she recognised as being of some of Petrogoria's most famous beauty spots. Woven silk rugs were scattered on gleaming wooden floors, and on a polished bureau she could see plenty of writing materials, along with golden pens in a jewelled container. A bowl of fruit stood on a low table and the two sofas which stood nearby were littered with soft and squashy cushions. Through a carved archway was a door leading to what was probably the bathroom and, beyond that, a wide and sumptuous-looking divan bed, scattered with yet more cushions. The bedroom, she thought, painfully aware of the sudden flush of colour to her cheeks as she prayed the bodyguard hadn't noticed.

'This all looks perfect,' she said, but suddenly all she could think of was how strange and alien it seemed. And how alone she was going to be for the next few weeks before the wedding—so far from home and away from everything which was familiar. She might moan about her family from time to time, but they were still her family, and right now they represented stability.

Constantin bowed. 'In that case, I will take my

leave of you, Your Royal Highness. Silviana is here to wait on your every need but if there is anything you discover you don't have—'

'I'm sure there won't be,' she said quickly.

'Anything it is within my power to give you,' he continued, as if she hadn't spoken, 'then please ring. At any time. I will be stationed directly outside your compartment.'

'You will?' questioned Zabrina nervously. 'Right outside?'

'But of course. Your welfare is my sole preoccupation and only a wall will divide us. Nobody will pass me to gain access to the Princess and I will remain awake for as long as the journey lasts.' He paused, his voice dipping. 'It is usually the custom for the chief bodyguard to eat meals with his or her royal subject.'

'Really?' she questioned.

'But of course. I need to taste your food and make sure it has not been poisoned, or tampered with. Which is why I am proposing to join you for dinner this evening, unless you have any objections to that.' Once again he flickered her a steely grey stare. 'Would such a proposition be acceptable, Your Royal Highness?'

Zabrina's mouth grew even dryer. She was expected to *eat meals* with him? She was expected to sit looking at his beautiful face, while all the time attempting to adopt an air of indifference? It sounded like a forbidden kind of heaven, made worse by the fact that Zabrina knew she shouldn't be thinking this way. She was promised to another man, wasn't she? That was the deal. She should be thinking about Roman and only Roman—beard or no beard. 'Why?' she questioned, playing for time. 'Am I such an unpopular choice to be your queen that I am likely to be poisoned?'

'Of course not.' He gave the faintest wave of dismissal. 'It is simply a necessary precaution. A safeguard, if you like, so that you will be delivered to the King unharmed.'

'I see,' said Zabrina slowly, but his use of the expression 'deliver' only reinforced the doubts she'd been experiencing earlier. Was that how *everybody* saw her—as a commodity? She supposed it was. She might be a crack shot who was fluent in four languages and thoroughly at home on the back of a temperamental horse. She might have devoted a huge portion of her time to working for women's charities and trying to get more equality for them in her homeland. But none of these things counted for anything, not really. And perhaps it was that which made a sudden streak of rebellion influence her decision, even though she had vowed to herself she wasn't going to make waves.

She could have told the autocratic bodyguard she wasn't particularly hungry and was quite happy to miss dinner—both of which were true. She could have hidden herself away in here and not seen anyone until they reached Rosumunte. But she wasn't going to. She glanced around at the sumptuous salon and suddenly it resembled nothing but a gilded cage.

Her gaze was drawn to the spring-like countryside outside—a blur of bright green as the train passed through. She was leaving her old life behind. When she returned here—and who knew when that would be?—it would be as the queen of a foreign country. One which had waged war against her ancestors in the past. And she was one of the spoils of that war. The modern-day virgin princess offered to the grisly king in exchange for a small chunk of his sizeable wealth.

Through the train window she caught a tantalising glimpse of an orchard at its very best. The branches of the trees were covered in thick white blossom, as if a mantle of snow had fallen on them. She found herself thinking of sunshine and birdsong and felt the sudden quickening of her blood.

Was it that which made her bold?

She was about to consign herself to a life of duty with the bearded King and, in essence, this was her last day of freedom. Surely she could have a little harmless fun before that happened? Would it be so wrong to mix socially with someone she wouldn't usually have been allowed anywhere near? Constantin Izvor obviously knew her husband-to-be as only a loyal servant could—and certainly a whole lot better than she did. Perhaps she could subtly learn a few tips on how best to handle the powerful King.

At least, that was what Zabrina told herself.

Just as she told herself it had absolutely nothing to do with the bodyguard's steely eyes and hard body.

'Yes, I suppose that will be okay,' she said carelessly, and then turned away before he saw the telltale flush in her cheeks.

CHAPTER THREE

As he stood outside the ornate door of the Princess's carriage, Roman felt the powerful thunder of his heart. His throat was dust-dry and his body tense as the train hurtled towards the vast forest which divided Albastase from Petrogoria. He felt excited, yes, but the familiar, blood-pumping sensation of desire which raced through his body was one which filled him with foreboding.

Because Princess Zabrina had thrown his thoughts into disarray and caused him to feel more than a little apprehensive. And, try as he might, he couldn't dispel the feeling that he had been short-changed. That he had somehow been misled about what to expect from his future bride.

He had anticipated a little more modesty from the virgin princess. For downcast lids to cover those forest-green eyes—not a challenging stare to be slanted in his direction, which had made the hairs on the back of his neck stand up. He found himself wondering if he had imagined the powerful sizzle of lust which had passed between them. Or had that simply been wishful thinking on his part—because he had looked at her and wanted her and suspected that she wanted him too, because women were never able to resist him? Had he misinterpreted her acerbic response as one of flirtation, when in reality she was genuinely irritated by him—hard as that might be to believe? He curved his lips into an indulgent smile. He would not judge her too harshly. Of *course* she wouldn't have been flirting with him—she would have known perfectly well that any such flirtation should be reserved solely for the monarch to whom she was promised.

But in a way, the fact he was having to ask these questions justified what he was about to do—for what better way to observe his future bride than through the invisible cloak of the humble servant? And when he revealed his true identity to her, he would do it in such a way that could not possibly offend. Even if she was piqued by his elaborate charade, any displeasure would quickly be smoothed away. He would charm her and shower her with the priceless gems he had brought with him and which were currently concealed within his carriage. Because jewels were always a reliable bargaining tool. He had observed the way women behaved with priceless and glittering baubles and doubted his bride-to-be would be any exception.

And he knew this princess was financially astute. Hadn't she already negotiated a fairly hefty personal settlement for herself within the terms of the marriage contract, which his lawyers had expressed some anxiety about? But her greed did not repel him. Instead, it reassured him. This marriage was nothing but a business deal and the Princess recognised that, too.

He rapped on the door and Silviana opened it. Of course she did. Did he really imagine that Zabrina herself would fling it open and ask him inside? He watched as the servant's brow creased above the line of her veil, and wondered if she was resisting the desire to curtsey to him. Probably. She knew his true identity but was too well trained to offer anything but a polite nod of greeting. Roman smiled. His equerry had obviously done his job well in warning the staff not to 'recognise' him. He glanced across to the other side of the room where a table had been set for dinner, right next to the window and the dusky countryside which was hurtling by. Pale, fragrant roses stood at the centre of the linen cloth and pure white candles had already been lit, casting flickering lights which contrasted with the darkening sky outside.

It was, he realised suddenly, a very romantic scene and now he found himself wondering if that was such a good idea.

Was he worried that temptation would assail him?

'The Princess will be with you shortly,' Silviana said. 'She is getting ready for dinner.'

He nodded, lifting the palm of his hand in a gesture of dismissal. 'Excellent. You may leave now, Silviana. We will ring the bell when we wish the meal to be served and after that I wish to be alone with the Princess for the rest of the evening.'

She hesitated for no more than a fraction of a moment but Roman had seen it and raised his eyebrows at her in arrogant query.

'Was there something else, Silviana?'

'No, no, not at all, Constantin Izvor,' she said hastily. 'Please. F-forgive me.'

But Roman barely registered the servant's stumbled apology or her silent departure. He was much too preoccupied by a growing sense of anticipation— an expectation which was allowed to mount during the thirty long minutes it took for Zabrina to arrive.

He was not used to being kept waiting. Nobody would dare make the King cool his heels in contemplation, and Roman quickly discovered he was not over-fond of the experience. He had often secretly wondered what it would be like to live as an ordinary man but was fast discovering that perhaps he had been guilty of sentimentalising a life of obscurity. Because this was *boring*—standing to attention while Zabrina took all the time in the world to prepare herself for dinner.

During the hours which had passed since she had closed the door on him earlier, he had allowed himself to fantasise about what she might choose to wear tonight. Was she dressing in one of her fine gowns to dine with him? he wondered, unable to prevent the sudden drying of his mouth. Would the soft rustle

of silk precede her, and that tanned skin be comple-
mented by the framing of lavish lace and satin? He
felt the heavy beat of desire as he imagined her pa-
rading around her bedroom in a variety of different
outfits, which banished his boredom just long enough
to ensure he was genuinely lost in thought when,
eventually, he heard a sound behind him. But there
was no rustle of silk or waft of fine perfume as he
turned round to survey his future queen.

Roman's lips parted in disbelief as the Princess
entered the salon.

Was this some kind of joke?

She had certainly changed from the embellished
dress she'd had on earlier but she had not replaced it
with something similarly splendid, or regal. No, she
was wearing a pair of what he believed were called
'sweatpants', teamed with a loose top which effec-
tively concealed her upper body like some kind of
monstrous, flapping tent. She had removed the pins
from her hair, too, but the intricate styling had not
been replaced by a gratifying fall of lustrous unfet-
tered hair. Instead, the thick brown locks were drawn
back in a tight ponytail and she looked...

His brow furrowed. She looked like a woman
leaving the gym!

She walked in and saw him and he observed
the wariness in her eyes. 'Oh,' she said, with that
same careless tone she'd used last time she'd spoken. 'You're here.'

'Did you think I wouldn't be?'

She shrugged. 'I wasn't sure.'

'I said I would be eating dinner with you, Your Royal Highness.'

'So you did. So you did. Well, you'd better stand at ease, I suppose.' She flopped down onto one of the sofas and Roman noticed her feet were bare and for some reason his disquiet was replaced by a mounting indignation that she should be so studiedly *casual* in his company. Because although she was ignorant of his royal identity—surely she shouldn't be so relaxed in the presence of a strange *male* bodyguard. Surely she shouldn't be stretching her arms above her head so that he couldn't help but be transfixed by the sudden pert outlining of her breasts beneath that horrible garment. Instantly, he looked out of the window and gave the darkening sky a searching scrutiny, as if scanning the horizon for potential threats. As if reminding himself that he was supposed to be guarding her and not running his gaze lustfully over her small and perfect body.

'Are we waiting for something?' she questioned.

'Not at all. I shall ring for dinner immediately,' he said, resenting the implicit order as he found himself noticing the curving sweep of her dark lashes which shuttered those amazing green eyes.

'You know, I'm almost tempted to ask if we couldn't have a sandwich or something instead,' she continued, huffing out a small sigh. 'At least that way we could cut the evening short.'

Again, people trying to limit the amount of time

they spent with him was something Roman wasn't used to. They usually hung on his every word until he took his leave of them, and he wasn't enjoying the sensation of knowing she was there under *sufferance*. No, he wasn't enjoying it one bit!

'A casual snack would of course be possible, Your Royal Highness,' he answered smoothly. 'Though surely you need to keep your strength up for the long days of celebration and preparation which lie ahead? I am certain that the royal chefs would be deeply disappointed if you didn't allow them to offer you a range of typical Petrogorian delicacies.'

The forest-green eyes were suddenly very direct. 'And is that to be my role for the evening?' she questioned quietly. 'That I am to moderate my behaviour in order to please the catering staff?'

'Of course not, Your Royal Highness,' he said stiffly. 'That was not what I meant.'

Zabrina saw the way the bodyguard's jaw tightened with obvious disapproval and in a way she couldn't blame him, because she probably *was* coming over as spoiled. But her behaviour was motivated more by self-protection, rather than petulance. She had been pacing her room restlessly ever since she had met Constantin Izvor at the beginning of this journey, glad to shut the door on him and mop her hand over her sweating brow. She had peeled herself out of her constricting gown and tried blaming *that* for the acute aching of her breasts and the increased sensitivity around the nipple area, which was making her feel oddly excited but deeply uncomfortable. She had convinced herself that if she dressed down in the comfy clothes she had secreted into her luggage without her mother's knowledge then she would quickly feel as relaxed as she sometimes did when she was gathered together with her sisters and brother, watching American films and eating popcorn in the palace games room.

But she had been wrong.

Despite the slouchy pants and baggy top, all those feelings of earlier were still there, only more so. In fact, she had only to look at the powerful bodyguard for her heart to start racing as if she had been galloping her horse at great speed.

But it was wrong to feel this way about the brooding servant. She was on her way to marry another man!

Conditioned by years of inbred royal etiquette, she sat up straight, put her shoulders back, pressed her knees together, and smiled as she tried to ignore the fake intimacy of the candlelit scene beside the window. 'Forgive me,' she said. 'I am not quite myself. This whole situation is so…'

His steely eyes narrowed. 'So what?' he questioned, as her words tailed off.

She shook her head. 'It doesn't matter.'

'But—'

'I said—' her voice was cool now, and properly regal '—it doesn't matter. And I meant it. Really, it

doesn't. So why don't you order supper, Izvor, because the sooner you do, the sooner I will be able
to retire for the night and you can go back to your
guard post?'

It puzzled her that a look of faint irritation crossed
his face and she wondered what on earth his agenda
was. Was he so arrogant about his undoubted good
looks that he found it hard to believe that a woman
would want to cut short her time with him? Maybe
she had been right in her initial assessment of wondering if his closeness to the King might have given
him ideas above his station. Or maybe he was dat-
ing one of the chefs and determined that their culi-
nary skills would be properly appreciated by the new
Queen! Was that why he seemed so determined to
have her eat an elaborate and possibly heavy meal
when that was the last thing she wanted?

And then the strangest thing happened and it took
her completely by surprise. A dark streak of something she didn't recognise shot through her body like
a sweeping arrow and Zabrina felt her chest tighten
as she imagined the bodyguard with another woman
in his embrace.

Hugging her.

Kissing her.

She swallowed as he reached for the bell, realising that the emotion was one of jealousy and that
she'd never felt it before. It unsettled her even more,
because surely to feel such an emotion about a ser-

vant was very, very wrong. 'I wonder, could you also organise something to drink for me?' she croaked.

'But of course. Is something the matter, Your Royal Highness? You look...' His steely eyes narrowed, as if he was suddenly remembering it was not his place to offer his opinion on how she looked. 'I trust you are not ill?'

'No, of course I'm not ill and nothing is the matter. I would just like a drink, if that's not too much to ask!'

She saw his brow darken with what was almost a scowl, before he replaced it with a bland smile.

'Of course, Your Royal Highness. Your wish is my command. Might I offer a little wine, perhaps? I could recommend a superb Petrogorian vintage, ma'am. Some say it is even finer than the finest of French wine—though obviously the French themselves are not among that number!'

Zabrina rarely drank alcohol—not even on high days and holidays—and, much as she longed for something which might help ease the terrible tension which was spiralling up inside her, she knew it would be foolish to accept a drink from Constantin Izvor. Because alcohol loosened the inhibitions—didn't it?—and instinct was warning her that was the *last* thing she needed to do right now.

'International comparisons between alcoholic beverages do not particularly interest me, if it's all the same to you,' she answered coolly. 'But I *would* like a drink of water.'

'Certainly, Your Royal Highness,' he said, a nerve working in his cheek as he rang the bell, as if he were having difficulty dealing with her testy orders. A manservant answered his summons and took the order, reappearing moments later, carrying drinks on a silver platter, before silently exiting the room.

She watched as Constantin poured sparkling water into a glass, lowered his head and sniffed it as though he were judging a fine wine and then solemnly sipped.

'Perfect,' he murmured, filling another crystal goblet and handing it to her, and as he did so his fingers brushed against her skin.

And Zabrina could do nothing about the shiver which whipped over her body, even though it angered her. Because wasn't it *insane* that such a brief touch could make her breath catch in her throat? How could something so small and so meaningless make her want to sit there gazing at him in rapt and eager wonder? She was behaving like a love-struck schoolgirl! Lifting up the glass, she took a mouthful, but even as the cool liquid quenched her parched throat all she could think about were the bodyguard's lips, which were gleaming in a way which was making her feel strangely stirred-up inside.

It was worrying.

It was more than worrying.

She was on her way to marry another man and all she could think about was the one standing before her.

More servants appeared, carrying plates and covered dishes, which were placed on the table, and once they'd gone Zabrina shot him a questioning look. 'You have dismissed the rest of the staff?'

He shrugged. 'The train carriage is relatively small, ma'am, and I suspected you would feel more relaxed if you were not being observed by your new subjects. Does my action not meet with Your Royal Highness's approval, for I can immediately rescind it if you would prefer?'

'No, no. That all sounds perfectly...reasonable.' She risked a glance into those pewter eyes and was immediately beguiled by their smokiness. 'Shall we sit?'

'If you don't mind, I would prefer to stand. And after I have sampled each dish, I will serve you.'

'Yes. Yes, of course,' said Zabrina hastily, terrified that she had broken some unknown rule of food-taster's etiquette. 'Thank you.'

Roman watched as she rose from her position on the sofa and slid onto one of the dining chairs, but as she shook out her napkin and placed it on her lap he thought she looked uncomfortable. As well she might, he thought grimly. She had casually invited him to sit opposite her—as if he were her equal! His mouth hardened. Was this how she *regularly* conducted herself when dealing with servants of the opposite sex—or with men in general? Were they unsuitably relaxed about such matters as correct social distancing, back at her palace in Albastase?

Briefly, he wondered if his judgment of her was unnecessarily harsh. He knew he possessed certain strong views about women and he knew, too, their source. But being aware of his own prejudices didn't mean he was going to blind himself to his future bride's obvious deficiencies!

He took his fork and ate some wild rice studded with pomegranates and pine nuts, and afterwards heaped a small amount on her golden plate, thinking that her tiny frame could surely not accommodate a larger portion than that.

He watched as she put a few grains into her mouth and found himself fascinated by the movement of her mouth as she chewed. It would be no hardship to kiss those soft lips, he thought, with a sudden fierce rush of desire, for he had not been intimate with a woman for well over a year, despite the many invitations which had come his way during his last royal tour. But he had resisted any such overtures, no matter how tempting they had been, aware that it would be unfair to the woman he was soon to marry if he had indulged in any pleasures of the flesh so close to their wedding.

But as a result, his sexual appetite was highly honed and keener than he could ever recall and he seemed to be growing harder by the second.

He cleared his throat. 'A little more, Your Royal Highness?'

'No, no. That was plenty.' She surveyed the selection of platters before her with a rueful smile. 'Especially as there appear to be several other courses to follow.'

He allowed himself a brief smile. 'Indeed there are.'

She lifted her head to look at him and, in the flicker of the candlelight, he was aware of feathery shadows on her honeyed skin, cast by her long lashes. 'Look, why don't you sit down for the rest of the meal, Constantin?' she said. 'It's hurting my neck to have to look up at you.'

Roman hesitated, but not for long, because it was a temptation too powerful to resist. It was a break with protocol, that much was true, but since he was planning to surprise her by revealing his identity before too long—and festooning her with a king's ransom in jewels—surely it wasn't too heinous a crime. Carefully, he removed his sword and put it within reach, before lowering his frame into the seat opposite hers. Then he forced himself to try and concentrate on the food he was tasting, rather than thinking how much he would give to free that magnificent mane of hair from its constricting ponytail and see what it looked like when it was tumbling down over her shoulders. But he comforted himself with the knowledge that it would not be too long before she was in his arms and in his bed. A few short weeks until their wedding and they could enjoy the legal consummation of their royal union. And if in the meantime, fuelled by his fierce hunger for her, that time passed with unendurable slowness, well, that wouldn't be the end of the world, would it? For wiser men than he had written that deprivation was a sure-fire guarantee of pleasure.

He forced himself to return his attention to the meal. Thin slivers of cold fish came next, accompanied by a leafy salad, soft with buttery avocado. She ate this with a little more interest and Roman experienced a small pang of compassion as, gradually, he saw her narrow shoulders relax and some of the tension leave her face and her body.

'You haven't eaten in a while,' he observed.

She looked up from her plate, her eyes narrowed and wary. 'How can you possibly know that? Are you a mind-reader or something?'

'That is one gift I suspect would be a double-edged sword,' he said drily. 'No, it's simply instinct. In the past I have commanded an army and can always recognise the signs when the men are hungry.'

'Oh?'

He shrugged, and as she continued to look at him curiously, he elaborated. 'Food is a necessity. A fuel, not a luxury, Your Royal Highness—although women often regard it as the enemy. And you need to eat. You're slim enough not to have to diet to get into your wedding dress and your brain and body need nourishment, especially when you consider what lies ahead.'

She put her fork down and he could see her lips

pressing in on themselves. 'If you don't mind, I'll skip the lecture,' she said. 'Though when I want advice on dieting or nutrition, I'll be sure to come to you.'

'Forgive me for my presumption.'

She bit down on her lip, as if she was itching to say something but trying very hard to hold her words back.

Which made Roman curious. Curious enough to let the silence between them grow into something very real and somehow brittle. He could feel a renewed tension in the air. He could see the distress clouding her forest-green eyes and all of a sudden the words came sliding from her mouth, even though he had not prompted them. Words he had not been expecting to hear, delivered with soft venom, as if she were excising a painful wound and needed all the poison to spill out before she could be healed.

'But what if you have no appetite?' she questioned in a low voice. 'What if you have barely been able to face food for days, because of the fate which awaits you?'

'To which fate do you refer, Your Royal Highness?' he questioned steadily. 'Surely your destiny is one which any princess would envy. Are you not about to become queen of one of the richest lands in the world and to marry its most powerful king?'

'Yes! Yes, I am,' she flared, putting her fork down with a clatter as she jumped to her feet. 'But unfortunately, that's the problem.'

'Problem?' he probed, his brow furrowed with confusion.

And now all semblance of protocol had disappeared and the face she turned towards him was both mulish with pride and pink with passion. 'Yes,' she breathed. 'A problem to which there is no satisfactory solution, for all my high-born position in life. Because I am being forced to marry a man I have no wish to marry!'

CHAPTER FOUR

ZABRINA WAS SHOCKED to find herself on her feet, staring across the table at Constantin Izvor as the train continued its swaying journey through the countryside. No, that wasn't quite true. She wasn't shocked. She was horrified.

Horrified.

Had she really just announced to the King's chief bodyguard that she had no desire to marry his esteemed boss?

Yes, she had. Guilty as charged.

So now what?

Trying to smooth her scrambled thoughts and work out how to get herself out of this bizarre situation, she walked over to the window to survey the darkening landscape outside. High up in the indigo sky the moon was nothing but a thin, almost unobtrusive slither, which meant that you could see the blaze of thousands of stars which bathed the countryside, illuminating the blossom-covered trees with an unworldly silver light. It was the most beautiful scene she could remember seeing in a long time, yet it felt unbearably poignant. She thought about the same stars shining high over her palace in Albastase and her brother and sisters assembled there, and was surprised by another wave of homesickness which swept through her.

But she couldn't be a coward. She must face the music she had managed to create all by herself. She had just committed what was, in effect, an act of treason. And if Constantin Izvor was determined to denounce her to his boss—which he was perfectly entitled to do—then she would have to accept her punishment and her fate.

Slowly, she turned around and lifted her gaze to his, but to her surprise the bodyguard did not look outraged. In fact, judging by the implacable expression on his devastatingly handsome face, he didn't even seem particularly shocked by what she had just blurted out. Just curious—the way she imagined someone might look if they had just been handed an envelope written in a hand they did not recognise.

'Look, can you forget you heard that?' she began falteringly. 'I was…overwrought. It must have been a lack of blood sugar—like you said.'

'Or not?' he negated.

She looked at him in surprise. 'Not?'

'In my experience, people don't just say things they don't mean. You clearly have some concerns—and concerns should always be addressed. So why don't I ring for these dishes to be taken away, while you go and sit down over there and compose your-self?' His grey eyes narrowed as he lifted the bell and rang it. 'And then perhaps I can put your mind at rest for you.'

He was gesturing towards one of the sofas on the opposite side of the salon and, once again, Zabrina thought he was behaving almost as if *he* were the host, rather than a member of the royal household! But by then a fleet of silent servants had arrived and were taking away all the used dishes, extinguishing candles and lighting soft lamps around the carriage, and by the time they had quietly shut the door behind them, she started thinking quickly. Wondering how she could possibly redeem herself in the light of such an inappropriate outburst, she sank onto the sofa he had indicated, thinking how blissfully comfortable it felt after being seated on that rather hard and ornate chair. Suddenly, the atmosphere seemed attractively inviting and *intimate*. She found herself wishing that the rest of the world would disappear and she could just stay in here, with him, protected and safe from the world. Wasn't that a bizarre thing to be thinking at such a time?

And now Constantin Izvor was moving across the silken rug towards her—this time not apparently requiring any invitation from her—and he sat down on the opposite end of the sofa and turned his head so that she was caught in the penetrating spotlight of that steely gaze.

'So,' he said, his accent sounding pronounced and

thoughtful. 'You clearly have reservations about your forthcoming wedding.'

She thought that was probably the understatement of the year. 'Doesn't every bride?' she hedged.

'May I ask why?'

It wasn't really a subject which should be up for discussion but there was something so…so *approachable* about the way he was looking at her that she found herself wanting to tell him, but something held her back. It would be far better to pretend they'd never started this conversation, wouldn't it? She could dismiss him and he would obviously obey and next time she saw him she could act as if nothing had happened. But that wouldn't work for all kinds of reasons. *He* would know what she'd said and he would either pass those words on to his boss, or keep them to himself. If he did the former she would be vilified, and the latter would mean there would be a big secret between the two of them which the King wouldn't be privy to. And both those outcomes would be a disaster.

So couldn't she backtrack a little? Play up her natural worries about marrying a man of the world like Roman, and make out that they were nothing but the natural fears of any innocent bride-to-be?

She lifted up her shoulders and felt her ponytail whispering against her back. 'I realise it came out all wrong—'

The brief shake of his head indicated his lack of agreement. 'It came out the way it did because it was something you were feeling at the time. But please be aware that I am not planning to judge you, Your Royal Highness, for it is not my place to do so. Or to tell tales,' he added coolly. 'I am simply interested in your reaction and thinking that perhaps you need to get something off your chest. Certainly before you arrive at the royal palace,' he concluded softly. 'For I know it can be an intimidating place at the best of times.'

'But I grew up in a palace!' she defended quickly. 'And I'm used to that kind of life.'

'Perhaps you are, but no palace in the world can equal the size or splendour of the Petrogorian citadel,' he said, eyeing her with a shuttered look. 'Look, why don't you consider me like a priest in the confessional, knowing that anything you say to me is bound by the rules of confidentiality and will go no further than these four walls?'

Anyone less like a priest, Zabrina couldn't imagine—because surely holy men weren't supposed to inspire thoughts of…of… She swallowed. Thoughts she didn't understand properly, but which were bubbling away inside her and making her want to squirm uncomfortably beneath his seeking gaze.

Yet hadn't one of her initial thoughts on meeting him been that he would know the King better than anyone? What better person to allay her fears about her future husband and put her mind at rest, than Constantin Izvor?

'I have heard that the King is very...ruthless,' she said at last.

His thin smile was followed by a shrug. 'Some might say that an element of ruthlessness is necessary for any monarch and particularly for a man as successful as Roman the Conqueror. He has increased our country's wealth by some considerable margin since coming to the throne, and brokered peace in a region which has a history of being notoriously unstable. As you know, Petrogoria has often come under siege from its neighbours in the past.' He flicked her a candid look. 'Including from your very own country, Your Royal Highness.'

Zabrina nodded. She wasn't going to defend the actions of her ancestors and their dreams of conquest—how could she, when they had planted the Albastasian flag on disputed territory, which they had claimed as their own and which was now being returned to its rightful owner?

'I know all that,' she burst out. 'I just wish I wasn't being offered up as the human sacrifice in all this! If you really want the truth, I wish I wasn't getting married to anyone—but certainly not to a total stranger.'

The look he shot her was pensive. 'But you will gain a massive financial package as a result of the marriage,' he observed. 'Plus, you understand all the privileges of royal life as well as its constraints. And do not most princesses want to marry a king?'

'It was a decision made for me by someone else.'

'Alas, that is one of the drawbacks and also one

of the strengths of an inherited monarchy. That the needs of the country are put ahead of personal need.'

'And the King is perfectly happy with this arrangement?' she questioned tentatively, thinking that *satisfactory* somehow sounded insulting.

'The King is governed by facts, not emotion. He knows perfectly well that a marriage of blue blood is preferable,' said Constantin, a sudden harshness entering his voice.

'The King's father married a commoner, didn't he?' probed Zabrina as she found herself remembering things she'd heard about him, and when he didn't answer, she persisted a little more. 'Was that one of the reasons why they had that terrible divorce? When he was so young? Didn't she leave, or something?'

The bodyguard's mouth twisted, as if he had just tasted something unspeakably sour. 'Something like that,' he agreed bitterly, before his face cleared and he looked at her with that oddly detached expression, as if it had been wiped clean of all emotion. 'Such an experience inevitably scarred him, but some say that boyhood pain makes for a powerful man.'

It was an aspect of the King's reputed character which Zabrina had never considered before, but there was another one which she had. One which naturally made her wary. 'Is he cruel?' she questioned suddenly.

He didn't answer straight away. His dark brow knitted together and his eyes narrowed, as if he had seen something outside on the horizon he wasn't sure he recognised. 'No.'

'You sound very sure.'

'That's because I am sure and, believe me, I know him better than anyone. It is true that some women have gone to the press and given interviews which imply cruelty,' he said eventually. 'But maybe that's because he has been unable to provide them with what they most desire.'

'And what do women most desire?' she questioned, into the silence which followed, feeling suddenly out of her depth.

'Can't you guess?'

'S-sex?' she questioned, with more boldness than she had ever displayed in her entire life.

'No, not sex,' he said softly, with a short laugh. 'Sex is easy.'

Zabrina blushed. 'What, then?'

'Love,' he said, and when she made no comment, he carried on. 'That nebulous concept which drives so much of the human race in hopeless pursuit and brings so much misery in its wake. I find that women are particularly susceptible to its allure. How about you?' He arched his black eyebrows questioningly. 'Do you rate love very highly, Your Royal Highness?'

'How would I know how to rate it when I have no experience of it?' she said quietly.

'Then you should consider yourself fortunate, for some say it is nothing but a madness and others do not believe in its existence at all,' he asserted, before giving his head a little shake. 'But forgive me, for I digress. I don't know how we got onto this subject. Were we not supposed to be talking about the King?'

'Yes,' she said, a little breathlessly. 'I suppose we were.'

'You will find Roman exacting and demanding at times, as most highly successful men are,' he continued. 'But he asks of people no more than he is prepared to give himself. He certainly drives himself too hard—his people often say that he defined the term *workaholic* before the word became widely used. But, at heart, he is a good man.'

Zabrina was aware that her lips had grown dry and that her heart had begun to skitter and suddenly her lack of desire to meet the King was growing. 'That's hardly the most glowing recommendation I've ever heard.'

'I am trying to be honest with you, Princess. Did you wish for me to spin you a fairy tale—to make him into the kind of man you would wish him to be? You are not being promised rainbows and roses, no, but something far more solid. You will be embarking on the tried and tested situation of the arranged marriage, which offers the highest chance of success.'

'And so, in order to guarantee this "highest chance", I am to be immersed in your culture, without outside influence. I am being taken to Petrogoria, without family or servants to comfort or reassure me. I am being prepared for your ruler, as a chicken would be prepared for the pot.'

She had spoken without thinking but, surprisingly, the comment made him laugh and Zabrina was shocked by how much that sexy sound affected her. It whispered over her skin like rich velvet. It made her want to curl up her toes and sigh.

'Ah, but an uncooked chicken is cold and lifeless,' he said softly as he removed his gun from its holster and laid it on the low coffee table in front of the sofa. 'While you are warm and very, very vibrant.'

The unexpected compliment shocked her and made her react in a way she hadn't been expecting. It made her breasts tighten beneath her sloppy sweatshirt and her heart begin to pound. She knew that what was happening was inappropriate, but somehow Zabrina had absolutely no power over what her body was doing. She looked into the steely gleam of his pewter eyes and felt a clench of something low in her gut. She'd experienced something like this a bit earlier, but this felt different. It was more powerful. It seemed to be eating her up from the inside and suddenly she was overcome with an aching regret that she would never know what it was like to be held within the powerful circle of Constantin Izvor's arms, or to be kissed by him.

She thought of all the photos she'd seen of her future husband. On horseback, wielding a sword. At an official function in New York with presidents and other dignitaries, or wearing a black tie and tuxedo at some glittering charity event. She'd seen images of him dressed in ceremonial robes and army uniform, and others of him working hard at his desk.

And not one of those images had provoked the faintest glimmer of desire in her.

'He's a grisly bear of a man,' she found herself whispering, dimly aware that Constantin's eyes were suddenly very bright and that he was actually sitting much closer to her than she'd thought. 'With a beard. And...'

There was a pause. A heartbeat of a pause.

'And?' he prompted smokily.

Zabrina looked at him and knew it still wasn't too late, even though she had already said far too much. She could send the bodyguard away and retire to her room and take whatever consequences came her way. But she couldn't seem to move. Not only couldn't, but didn't want to, despite the undeniable thrum of danger in the air and the sense that something momentous was about to happen. She just wanted to sit there, drowning in the smoky grey light from his eyes and letting his velvety voice wash over her. 'And I hate beards,' she added, her voice suddenly fierce.

Roman nodded in response to her bitter words. He should have been angry. It was surely his *right* to be angry but that was the last thing he was feeling. Maybe because the defiant face which was turned to his was so irresistible. Maybe because he wasn't used to such candour, not from anyone. He could see the urgent flicker of a pulse beating at the base of her

neck and could sense all the latent resentment which
had stiffened her slender frame. But there was something else he could see in her eyes and that something
was desire—a sexual hunger which surely matched
the one which was pulsing around his veins. It had
been present from the moment they'd met and now
it was plainer than ever.

She didn't want the man she was promised to, he
realised—and yet she wanted *him*.

He shook his head slightly, knowing what he
should do. He should immediately absent himself
from her company and address the disturbing aspects of her character this had raised in the cold,
clear light of morning. But he knew he wasn't going
to. He was going to kiss her. He *had* to kiss her because she was drawing him to her like a magnet. He
was dazzled by the light which shone from her eyes.
As he looked into her face his overriding sensation
was one of intoxication. Or maybe he had just been
celibate for too long and was woefully unprepared
for any kind of temptation.

All he could see was the gleam of her lips. The
rise and fall of her breasts and the whisper of her unsteady breath as she looked at him, those forest-green
eyes soft and molten with hunger. The subtle scent of
desire hung like a musky perfume in the air and he
felt it wrapping him with silken bonds. He knew he
should tell her the truth. Tell her who he really was.
But how could he possibly explain his dilemma when
right then he wasn't sure *who* he was? No longer an

ice-cold monarch or masquerading bodyguard, but a man whose senses had been invaded with a potency which had taken him by surprise, leaving his nerve-endings clamouring and urgent with need.

It felt visceral.

It felt all-consuming.

As if everything he'd ever known before that moment had been forgotten and was focussed in the hard, sweet throbbing at his groin.

He must have moved, for his shadow threw her slender body into shaded relief and his face hovered above her startled, yet hungry expression. And suddenly he was responding to the glint of invitation in her eyes. He was bending to brush his lips over hers, fired up by the groan of pleasure which passed from her mouth to his as he kissed her. He told himself that any moment now she would come to her senses and push him away, but that wasn't happening. Her fingers were on his shoulders. They were digging into his flesh and she was pulling him closer, as if she wanted him to go deeper. And he did. God, he'd never kissed a woman as deeply as this before. The pressure of their seeking mouths was like lighting the touchpaper of a firework. He could feel her breasts pressing against his chest. His tongue laced with hers and she was moaning softly—moaning like someone in the middle of an erotic dream who was just about to come.

Was she?

Or was *he*?

Maybe.

Roman slipped his hand beneath her baggy top and a groan of pleasure escaped him as he cupped her breast in his palm, luxuriating in the lace-covered feel of it. He kneaded the soft flesh, thinking how much more luscious it was than it had appeared beneath her embellished dress of earlier. He grazed a negligent thumb over one pert nipple and heard her little moan of joy.

His lips on her neck, he ran the tip of his tongue over her skin and felt her shiver in response and, as he tasted her flesh, he felt utterly bewitched by her. His hand moved down towards the waistband of her sweatpants and she was circling her hips towards him, like a dancer on a podium inviting men to throw money at her. And all the questions he should have asked—not just of himself, but of her—suddenly seemed to evaporate.

Hadn't he told her that everything which was said would remain between these four walls for ever— and didn't that count for everything they *did*, as well?

'Princess,' he intoned huskily. But it was more than an undeniable purr of appreciation. It was also an unspoken question which they both understood as he stared deep into her eyes.

Zabrina stilled as she heard the use of her official title, but even that brief brush with reality wasn't enough to dampen her desire for him, which was off the scale. He was tacitly asking if she wanted to continue and she knew only too well what she ought to say. Despite her inexperience, she could sense that things were getting rapidly out of control, yet she was doing nothing to stop him—and it was pretty obvious why. All during dinner she'd been fascinated by him. She had been deeply attracted to him on a physical level, yes, but there had been a huge element of trust, too.

He had told her she could confide in him and for some reason she had believed him—because the light shining from his grey eyes had looked genuine and honest. So she had. She'd told him more than she'd ever told anyone. But all those confidences now seemed like a double-edged sword. It had been good to get things off her chest and vocalise her doubts to someone outside her immediate family, yet the freedom of doing such an *unroyal* thing had made her feel strangely restless and…incomplete.

It had made her long for the freedom to do more of the same. It had made her wish she weren't a princess who was being sold off to a man she didn't know, but a woman who had the ability to make her own choices about things. Like, about who she would give her body to, when she chose to have sex for the first time. Constantin had tried to put her mind at rest by explaining that Roman was an *exacting* rather than a cruel king—but that didn't cancel out the fact that she didn't fancy him, did it?

But she fancied Constantin.

Her heart pounded almost painfully. She fancied him more than she could say. Especially as he was now peeling back her sweatshirt and bending his mouth to the mound of her breast. She tipped her head back and a helpless shudder ran through her as he sucked at the nipple through the flimsy barrier of her new bra. And now he was beginning to stroke her belly and she wanted more. Much more. She could feel the molten heat building between her thighs, along with a hungry pulse of need which had started flickering there. Her mouth dried to dust because he was igniting a yearning deep inside her and it felt so incredible that every cell of her body was screaming to let him carry on.

So she did.

She told herself it would only be for a minute. Certainly no longer than that.

His hand slipped further down and he pushed aside the centre panel of her panties, which were almost shockingly wet, and Zabrina gave a little cry as he made contact with her aching flesh. She swallowed. Was it so wrong for his finger to be skating urgently over that most intimate part of her? And for that same finger to alight on the exquisitely sensitised nub before beginning to move in delicate rhythm? How could it be wrong when it felt like nothing she'd ever experienced before? When it felt so *good*…

She closed her eyes as the light movement made her catch her breath, then blindly she lifted her face to his, and his responding kiss made her feel as if she were drowning in honey.

'Princess?' he groaned again against her lips.

Again she sensed that some new barrier was about to be crossed and he was seeking her permission. Maybe if he'd said her name then common sense might have prevailed, but his repetition of her title made her feel slightly disconnected and uncaring of the consequences. As if this were not happening to her but to someone else—someone she didn't know very well. A wild stranger who was briefly inhabiting her body and demanding that this fierce sexual hunger be fed.

'Yes,' she said, in her own language, her next words muffled by the sweatshirt he was pulling over her head. 'Yes, please.'

CHAPTER FIVE

HE WAS UNDRESSING. Or at least, he was freeing himself from his clothes. There was very little ceremony involved. Zabrina watched as Constantin Izvor impatiently removed his long leather boots and kicked them aside, before peeling off his dark trousers and sending them in the same direction, after first extracting a mysterious packet of foil.

His shirt followed, exposing the honed magnificence of his bare chest—but there wasn't really time to appreciate it because the bodyguard was turning his attention to her once more. He splayed his palms over her hips, her slouchy pants were swiftly disposed of and it wasn't until she felt the rush of cool air against her legs that it suddenly occurred to Zabrina that Constantin was completely naked, while she was still wearing her underwear.

His eyes narrowed as if he had suddenly tuned into her thoughts. 'We don't seem to be very equally matched,' he murmured.

It was almost enough to destroy the mood, because Zabrina knew they would *never* be equally matched, because, no matter how vaulted his position, he was still a servant and she a royal. But by then she didn't care, because he was deftly unclipping her bra and her reservations were dissolved by the delicious sensation of her breasts sliding free. She liked the way that made her feel, just as she liked the way his eyes had darkened in response.

His gaze roved to the only remaining barrier to her nakedness—a tiny triangle of pink lace panties, which matched the bra—and she saw his mouth harden with something she didn't recognise. Something which looked faintly disapproving. Surely not—for hadn't part of her pre-wedding sexual education reinforced the fact that men liked provocative lingerie and it was a wife's duty to heed such desires?

Zabrina chewed on her lip. Perhaps he was perplexed by her extravagant underclothes, particularly when worn underneath such a deliberately unglamorous outer layer. She wondered what he'd say if he knew that the flimsy garment was completely unlike the sleek black briefs she normally favoured, which made horse-riding so much easier.

But now was not the time to start thinking about the trousseau which had been acquired by one of her mother's stylists. Not when he was hooking the sides of her panties with his fingers while making a low, growling noise at the back of his throat. For one crazy moment she thought he was about to rip them off and wasn't there an unknown and rather shocking side to her character which actually hoped he *would*? But she had been mistaken, because he was removing them conventionally enough, sliding them down over her knees—though with hands which were slightly unsteady.

His watchful eyes burned into her as he ran a questing finger over her thighs, lightly stroking the goose-pimpled flesh in inciting circles which made them tremble even more. And suddenly Zabrina found herself parting her legs for him, as if his pewter gaze was compelling her to do so—and he was…he was…

She gave a startled gasp as Constantin Izvor bent his head down between her thighs. His tongue began to dart over the exquisitely aroused flesh and he gently hushed her with a single, 'Shh!'

It was an impossible order. How could she possibly stay silent when he was working such magic? When he was making her feel like this—as though she were rapidly soaring towards an unknown destination? Some place of unbelievable sweetness which was beckoning to her with honeyed fingers. It felt shockingly intimate. Decadent and delicious. It felt *perfect*.

Helplessly, Zabrina writhed beneath the featherlight accuracy of his tongue, scarcely able to believe that it could get any better. But it did. It was getting better all the time. It was so good that she felt as if she were going to faint with pleasure. She bit back a cry of disbelief mingled with joy, and just as her body started convulsing he pressed his lips against her pulsating core. Bunching up her fist, she dug her teeth hard into her fingers and bit on them as the flick of his tongue intensified the blistering sensations. One delicious spasm was followed by another and never had she felt quite so vulnerable—or so powerful— as she did in that moment. Time stretched and suspended and she found herself strangely reluctant to float back down to earth.

Her eyelids parting, she saw Constantin opening the foil packet he'd retrieved earlier and Zabrina suddenly understood what it contained. She'd never even seen a contraceptive before—why would she?—and she'd always imagined she might feel a mixture of terror and embarrassment when eventually she did. But the only thing she was experiencing right now was a warm anticipation as he moved to lie on top of her. His flesh was silky and hard. She could feel the muscled weight of his body and his satin tip nudging against the core he had just kissed so intimately. She could detect a faint perfume in the air, and as he lowered his head to kiss her she could taste the scent on his tongue and realised that the taste was *her*.

'Constantin,' she said, almost brokenly.

'What?'

For a moment she felt him grow still against her, as if he was having second thoughts.

Was he?

Should *she* be having them?

Of course she should.

A lingering remnant of common sense reminded her of the insanity of what she was about to do—yet her body was so greedy for more of this incredible pleasure that it refused to contemplate any other alternative than what was about to happen.

'What is it?' he demanded again, his voice raw and ragged with need.

'N-nothing.' If she wasn't careful she would start putting doubts in his mind, and the King's servant would realise what a compromising position they were in. And if he decided to call a halt to it could she really bear it? No, she could not. Was that what made her instinctively thrust her pelvis forward, so that his tip entered by a fraction and he gave a soft roar as he thrust into her more deeply?

Zabrina sucked in a disbelieving breath as he filled her and she was amazed at how quickly her body adjusted to his possession—as if she had been waiting all her life for this man to be inside her. She let out a slow shudder as he began to move and, very quickly, could feel an escalation of that now-familiar bliss with each powerful thrust he made. But as his mouth fixed itself on hers and she felt the lace of his tongue again, she suddenly became aware that this was about more than the purely physical. It felt as if the two of them really had become one—in every sense. Did she feel that connection because he'd convinced her to confide in him? Or because he'd made her feel almost normal—less like a princess and more like a woman?

And that had never happened before.

'Oh,' she whimpered.

He raised his dark head, his eyes seeming unfocussed. 'Oh, what?'

'It feels…amazing.'

'I know it does.'

What was that sudden edge to his voice as he drove even deeper? Zabrina wasn't sure but right then she didn't particularly care, because it seemed that instinct was guiding her movements again. Why else did her thighs lock with familiar ease around his back, and why else did she move her pelvis to meet each hard thrust? The low moans of pleasure he gave thrilled her immeasurably. Did that mean he liked the way she was responding to him? She hoped so because she liked everything he was doing to her.

Everything.

She liked the way his teeth teased her nipples into diamond points. The way he smoothed his fingers over her arching flesh, as if discovering every centimetre of her body through touch alone. Each thrust he made took her deeper, and then deeper still, into a new and intoxicating world which was becoming familiar to her. In her befuddled mind she saw the twitch of a colourless curtain, behind which was a glimpse of that rainbow place again. And suddenly it became real, and all those incredible sensations were swamping her in tantalising waves.

It couldn't be happening, Zabrina thought dimly. Not...not again.

But it could, and it was.

Oh, it *was*.

As her body began to clench around him, he drove his mouth down on hers—as if recognising that kissing was the only way of stemming the euphoric cry which was bubbling up inside her. Zabrina yelped softly into his mouth as his movements became more urgent—until at last he jerked inside her, his head tipping back as he shuddered out his own moment of fulfilment.

It felt like an intensely private moment but she was so dazed and spellbound that she risked a glance at his face.

He looked enraptured. There was no other word for it. As if he'd just discovered the most delicious thing imaginable. And for a few silent seconds, Zabrina allowed herself the pointless luxury of fantasy.

What if he'd realised—like her—that this type of connection was rare? So rare that she would be prepared to give up her destiny for it. For him. She could tell him that she'd meant what she'd said about his boss—that she had no desire to marry him, nor even any desire for him. She could renounce her royal title and they could run away together. There would be

a terrible scandal, yes, but people would get over it
and the world would move on. He was strong and
resourceful. He could build them a cottage in the
woods and she would bear his children. She would
cook meals and grow vegetables and he would come
home every night and take her into his arms, and...
She frowned. It was true that she'd never cooked anything in her life, but she would soon learn!

'Constantin,' she said softly, and as she said his
name an astonishing transformation seemed to come
over him.

The first thing he did was to withdraw from her,
as if he couldn't wait to put some distance between
them. But not before she'd detected the way he had
begun to harden inside her once more...and she
sensed he was having to fight the urge not to thrust
inside her again. She wished he would. She wanted
to ask him if something was wrong but her inexperience warned her to wait a little. Because he might be
awash with feelings of guilt and regret at what they'd
just done—feelings she knew she should share, but
somehow she just couldn't. How on earth could she
possibly feel guilty or regretful about something
which felt as if it had been written in the stars?

His back to her now, he peeled off the condom
and dropped it on top of his discarded trousers, as
if this was something he had done a million times
before. He probably had, Zabrina reasoned, though
she needed to understand that his life before he'd

met her was none of her business and she must not question him about it. Not when they had more than enough questions of their own they needed to address. In fact, he was probably wondering where the hell they went from here, so surely it was up to her to put his mind at rest and reassure him that she wasn't intending to pull rank.

'Constantin?' she repeated softly.

He turned to face her then and Zabrina almost wished he hadn't, because...

Surely there had to have been some kind of mistake? Surely someone couldn't have travelled from bliss to contempt so quickly. But eyes which had been soft and smoky with lust now resembled chips of grey ice and his face looked as if he had pulled on a dark mask of anger. Was he anticipating the repercussions of what they had done?

She frowned. 'Is...is something wrong?'

'What do you think?' he snapped, his voice as cold as his eyes.

She swallowed. 'I know we shouldn't have—'

Roman shook his head, unable to contain his anger for a second longer. Anger at the naked princess who was still tempting him unbearably, yes, but far more potent was the anger he was directing at himself. How could he have lost control like that? How *could* he? 'Damned right, we shouldn't,' he snarled.

She was sitting up in bed and smoothing down her

hair, shiny strands of which were tumbling from its constricting ponytail and falling tantalisingly over her bare breasts.

'Look, I don't have any experience but I do know that these things happen,' she whispered.

Her wide-eyed expression was completely at odds with the foxy euphoria he'd witnessed when she'd been orgasming underneath him and now Roman felt another spear of anger directed at the erection which was stirring at his groin. 'Oh, please. Don't insult my intelligence by playing the wounded innocent, when nothing could be further from the truth!'

She blinked at him in confusion and it almost looked real. She was a good actress, he'd say that for her.

'What are you talking about, Constantin?'

The way she spoke his name made another wave of anger wash over him. 'What do you think I'm talking about?' Furiously, he rose from the bed and grabbed at his clothes, rapidly pulling on his trousers before heading towards the bedroom at the far end of the compartment. From there, he tugged a silken coverlet from the bed and walked back into the salon before tossing it to her. 'Cover yourself up,' he said, striding over to the door and turning the key in the lock.

Thankfully, she did as he asked, concealing her delicious body from his hungry eyes with the aid of the bedspread. That was one less distraction at least,

Roman thought grimly as a pert pink nipple was covered by a ripple of silk, though he couldn't deny his faint sense of deprivation. His mind was buzzing but all he could see was the fearful gaze she was directing at the door before looking back at him, as if she had only just realised where they were and what they had been doing.

'Oh, my goodness. We could have been discovered,' she was breathing in horror. 'Anyone could have walked in at any time.'

Roman shook his head. He had been wondering how he could tell her what she needed to know—he just hadn't been sure how to go about it. But now he was. There was a perfectly simple way of alerting her to the simple fact which was going to change her fate for ever. His, too. Yet wasn't there a part of him which felt a kind of *relief* at the prospect that he would no longer need to marry her? No need to marry *anyone*.

'Nobody would have walked in,' he declared, with icy certainty.

She gave a nervous laugh. 'You can't possibly know that.'

'Yes, I can.'

'How?'

The stab of conscience he had all but eliminated made another brief attempt to unsettle him, but Roman quickly quashed it. Because surely her deception was far greater than his? He looked into her forest-green eyes and sucked in a deep breath.

'Because my name is not Constantin Izvor and I am not the chief bodyguard to the royal household. I am—'

'You are the King,' she interrupted suddenly, her face growing as white as a summer cloud. 'You are King Roman of Petrogoria.'

CHAPTER SIX

'HOW THE HELL do you know who I am?' he demanded.

Zabrina felt a flicker of pleasure that she'd taken him by surprise because surely her sudden realisation of the King's true identity gave her back a modicum of control over this awful situation.

But only a modicum.

Keep cool, she told herself fiercely, as the train continued to rattle through towards the border which divided their two countries. Don't let him guess at your thoughts or your feelings. Because if he does— *if he does*—that will give him even more power than he already possesses. If he realised, for example, that her primary feeling was one of hurt and betrayal, then wouldn't that run the risk of making her appear even more foolish? She shuddered as she forced herself to recall her stupid imaginings. Had she seriously been considering renouncing her title and her life to live in a country cottage with him? She must have been out of her mind.

'How long have you known my true identity?' he questioned coldly.

She forced herself to glare at him instead of drinking in his steely beauty, which she had been doing until just a couple of minutes ago. Why, if she was capable of winding the clock back even by a minute, she would still be in that dazed place of sensual fulfilment, her body all glowing and tingly. And wasn't it crazy that, even now, she was finding it difficult to remain immune to his physical allure? It was very difficult to concentrate on anything when she noticed he'd left the top button of his trousers undone. 'You mean, how long is it since I found out that you've been deceiving me, since even before I boarded this royal train?'

'You dare to talk to me of deception?' he flared back. 'When you were planning to arrive in my country to great fanfare and acclaim and then to marry me, having had sex with someone you believed was my bodyguard?'

Zabrina felt completely wrong-footed by his icy accusation, which was presumably his intention—because everything he'd said was true. She *had* done all those things. But it was all becoming much clearer now. When she had met the man who had introduced himself as Constantin Izvor, she had quickly noticed his autocratic bearing and had thought he was a little full of himself. *Of course he was.* He had been trying to behave like a commoner, when all his life he had occupied one of the most powerful positions in the region. No wonder he had struggled with humility. No wonder he had such strong traces of arrogance. She had thought that at times he seemed almost regal—because he was! Oh, why hadn't she trusted her instincts and found out more about him, instead of taking everything he said at face value? Why the *hell* had she trusted him? Hadn't she learnt ever since she was barely out of the cradle that men were selfish creatures who were not to be trusted?

'You started it!' she declared. 'You started the whole seduction process!'

'How?'

'By telling me…' Oh, how trite it sounded now and how gullible she had been. 'By telling me that my skin was soft and silky—'

'And do you respond to all men who compliment you like that?' he snapped. 'If, say, one of the servants had admired the colour of your eyes, would he have been allowed to put his head between your thighs and be in the position I now find myself in?'

'How dare you?'

'It's a simple question, Zabrina. All it needs is a yes or a no!'

'I shouldn't even dignify that question by responding, because you know very well what the answer is. The answer is no, of course it is. Because I was an innocent,' she elaborated, when he continued to look at her coldly.

'What the hell,' he iced out, 'are you talking about?'

Zabrina had thought it couldn't possibly get any worse than it already was, but she had been wrong. She looked at the contemptuous curve of his lips and a terrible truth began to dawn on her—one so awful that initially she wouldn't allow herself to believe it. Surely he didn't think…? 'I was a virgin,' she repeated—and wasn't it another stupid side-effect of the situation she now found herself in that she should feel embarrassed about having a clinical discussion about something so personal, when in his arms she had behaved completely without inhibition?

'Oh, please.' His laugh was bitter. 'We may have both committed the sin of deception, but that time has gone, and from now on perhaps we should agree to speak only the truth.'

'That's exactly what I am doing.'

'I'm giving you time to think about what you've just said and to modify it accordingly. You were no virgin, Princess. So please don't insult me by pretending that you were!'

Instinctively, Zabrina's fingers dug into the silken coverlet as his gaze raked over her and she wondered if she had imagined that sudden brief darkening of his eyes. Was that because she was naked underneath it? she wondered. And did he still want her as much as she wanted him? How inconvenient desire could be, she thought bitterly, aware of her hardening nipples in response, and the molten heat which clenched so tantalisingly at the base of her belly. 'Are you saying I *lied* to you about my inexperience?'

'If it makes you feel better, I'll be generous and put it down to you being creative with the facts. I can understand your reasoning because obviously you want to protect your reputation. But it won't make me think any worse of you if you admit to the truth,' he added. 'It certainly won't change the outcome of what I am about to do next.'

Maybe she should have addressed the slightly sinister portent of 'what I am about to do next', but Zabrina was so horrified by his accusation that she briefly forgot his words. 'Why are you saying that?' she whispered, and then, as a sudden horrified thought sprang into her mind, she glanced over at the sofa to quickly put her mind at rest, relieved to see that it was as pristine as before. 'Because there was no evidence? Were you hoping to fly the bloodied sheet from the palace balcony in Rosumunte on our wedding night? Aren't we royals supposed to have moved on from those days?'

'Please do not try to distract me with inappropriate sarcasm!' He glowered at her. 'Because I *know* how a woman behaves when it is her first time with a man. She is shy. She is tentative. She is often overwhelmed by what is happening to her.'

'How encyclopaedic you sound, *Roman*. Which

leads me to conclude that you must have had sex with many virgins before?''

'Some.' He shrugged. 'Not many.'

'And is that supposed to make me feel better?'

'I don't imagine anything would be able to do that at the moment,' he commented wryly and gave a sudden, heavy sigh. 'But if it's any consolation, I feel pretty much the same.'

'It isn't!' she snapped. 'I'm not interested in consolation, even if you were capable of providing any, which I suspect you aren't. And as for knowing how a woman behaves when it is her first time—don't you suppose that any shyness on her part might have something to do with the fact that you're a powerful king? Except when you're pretending not to be, of course.' She gave a short laugh. 'Surely your crime was worse than mine, since you knew exactly who I was. Was that your intention all along, *Roman*? To seduce me? Was this some sort of primitive test of my character to see how much temptation I could take before submitting to you?'

'Which I have to say you failed quite comprehensively, Princess.'

'Well, maybe you shouldn't be so skilled at seduction!'

There was silence for a moment before eventually he expelled a long sigh. 'Look, I can see with hindsight that it's unreasonable of me to apportion blame,' he said, lifting the palms of his hands in what looked like a gesture of conciliation.

'Why don't you say that as if you mean it?' she demanded, thinking that here was a man who was a stranger to the word *apology*. But weren't all powerful men like that—especially kings? They only said sorry if they were forced to—the way her father had done in the past, when he'd been found out in his latest dalliance. They might go through the motions, but they never really *meant* it.

'I have had sexual partners before,' he continued. 'So I guess it's not unreasonable that you should have done the same.'

'But?' She raised her eyebrows. 'I sense there's a "but" coming.'

Again, a shrug—but this time there was no accompanying hint of apology. 'We both know that the unwritten clause in our marriage contract is that you should have known no lover other than me, Zabrina. It's how these things work. Sexual equality may be alive and well in most of the world, but it has yet to reach either of our two countries. And I'm certain your grasp of royal history is thorough enough for you to realise that there can be no possible question over the legitimacy of any future progeny, which can only be the case if my bride is pure.'

'Pure?' Zabrina stared at him, tugging the band from her hair and giving her ruffled mane an angry shake. 'Look, believe or don't believe that I wasn't

the cowering little innocent you were hoping for—I don't particularly care either way. But please don't illustrate your prejudices with such ridiculous euphemisms. You make me sound like a bar of soap!'

For a moment Roman almost smiled at her outburst, until he remembered the gravity of the situation in which he now found himself. A situation which must be resolved as quickly as possible. He shook his head. If only he could just walk out of the salon now and pretend that this had all been like a bad dream.

Or an irresistibly sweet one…

But he couldn't. That was the trouble. Nobody could rewrite the past, no matter how much power they possessed at their fingertips. And unfortunately, the past wasn't his only dilemma—not when the present was haunting him in a way he hadn't anticipated. He found himself wishing she were someone else. Someone anonymous, with whom he had no projected future, so that he would have no qualms about going back over to the sofa on which she reclined and ravishing her over and over again as he hungered to do. What wouldn't he give to feel her soft thighs wrapped around his back one more time, and hear her soft moans of joy as he thrust into her with wild abandon? He swallowed, looking into her defiant face and realising she didn't look in the least bit *chastened*—which he might have expected in the circumstances.

Until he forced himself to remember that this was not a virginal princess who was grateful to marry the mighty King who had been selected for her. No, this was a princess who had betrayed, not only him, but both their lands. And now she would pay the ultimate price for her folly.

Yet he remembered what it had felt like to touch her and he felt a bitter regret that he would never experience it again. Sex had never felt like that before. As if he would die if he didn't possess her. As if his very life had depended on being deep inside her. He remembered the battle which had raged within him as he'd fought to conquer the terrible desire she had unleashed in him. To stop what was happening before it reached the point of no return. But he had been unable to turn away from her sweet temptation and prevent himself from stripping them both bare, before losing himself in her delicious honey. As he had entered her, he had looked deep into her eyes and seen a powerful yearning which had matched his own and a random thought had briefly speared his mind. A thought which contradicted everything he had been brought up to believe.

That this woman was his equal.

But he forced himself to focus on the truth instead of fantasy.

Yes, she was a woman who would have made a superb mistress.

But a thoroughly unsuitable wife.

He wondered if she would save face by exiting their embryo relationship with the minimum of fuss or whether she needed him to spell it out for her. He thought perhaps she did since she was studying him with an impassive expression, almost as if nothing had changed. When everything had changed.

But he knew that this was a delicate situation which required careful and diplomatic handling, if the fallout was to be kept to a minimum.

'You have many attributes, Princess,' he said slowly. 'You are a beautiful and intelligent woman and I am certain you will find another man who is willing to marry you. Perhaps not one as highly connected as I am, it is true.' He glimmered her a smile, trying to reassure her, yes, but also trying to convince himself that nothing would be gained from making love to her again. He tried to take his mind off his throbbing groin. 'And you must rest assured that what I said earlier was true. Nothing which has passed between us will go any further than these four walls.' He gave her a swift, businesslike smile. 'Your secret will be safe with me.'

Some of the impassivity left her face. 'My...secret?'

'Nobody will ever know what happened between us, Princess. It will be like closing the chapter of a book.'

Zabrina flinched and not just because his words were filling her with fury, but because they were managing to turn her on at the same time. How did he *do* that? For a few brief seconds she felt almost powerless over the effect his cool stare was having on her. Why else would she find herself recalling how amazing it had felt to have him peeling off her panties? Or remembering the expert flick of his tongue against her throbbing bud until he had brought her to orgasm? She swallowed as she remembered the second orgasm when he'd been deep inside her. Just the thought of what he'd done was making her stomach dissolve and her skin grow heated. Surely, if she wasn't careful, he would guess at the effect he was having on her.

And that was something she simply couldn't afford to let happen.

Setting her mouth into a firm line, she stared at him. 'You mean, you are no longer planning to marry me?' she verified.

His sigh sounded genuinely regretful—it was just a pity the steely glint of relief in his eyes didn't match the sentiment. 'I cannot marry you, Princess—for the reasons I have already expanded upon and which I am sure you understand. Because if you are being honest with yourself, can you really be hypocritical enough to exchange public vows with a man you theoretically betrayed, even before you'd met him?'

'I—'

'The wedding must be called off as quickly as possible. We just need to work out the best way to go about it and how best to return you to your country.' A new and gritty note entered his deep voice. 'A damage-limitation exercise, if you like.'

If she *liked*?

Zabrina could hardly comprehend the audacity of the man. How did he have the nerve to start talking about *damage limitation* and coolly state that he was about to send her back to Albastase like some reprimanded schoolgirl? She bristled with indignation. And wasn't it funny how contrary human nature could be? Earlier that day she would have sold off the few humble jewels she possessed if someone could have guaranteed her a get-out clause for her marriage to the grisly King.

Except that he wasn't grisly.

He was anything but. He was gorgeous enough for her to have eagerly surrendered her virginity to him—a virginity he didn't believe she'd possessed. So not only had he deceived her, he had also accused her of lying! His list of crimes against her was long, but could she afford to dwell on them, or take offence? No, she could not. She needed to keep her eye on the bigger picture and not on whether or not her feelings were hurt, because at the end of the day that didn't matter. Feelings passed. They waxed and waned like the moon whose cold, silver crescent now looked like a scythe hanging outside the train window.

She thought about the different choices which lay

ahead of her. She and Roman could agree a joint statement which could be put out by both their countries, stating that the wedding would not take place. They could fudge a reason—although it was difficult to see what that reason might be. Incompatibility was hardly going to work as a believable concept, because the underlying understanding within an arranged marriage was that compatibility had to be *worked* at.

She swallowed. Then there was all the expense involved—all the lavish celebrations which would need to be cancelled—not to mention the disappointment of their subjects, who were looking forward to a three-day holiday of feasting and dancing, once the wedding had taken place. But those things paled into insignificance when she remembered the real purpose behind this union…

Her country badly needed an injection of funds to bring it back from the brink of economic ruin.

And wasn't she the only person who could do it?

If the wedding was called off, she would be seen as a failure. No matter how they spun it she would always be known as the Jilted Princess, unwanted by the highly desirable and powerful ruler. She would be the one who would be judged negatively, because in this region men were seen as more important than women. Her father would be furious that she had failed to provide the goose that laid the golden egg, but ultimately wouldn't it be her brother and her sisters who suffered as a result of a cancelled marriage?

Zabrina sucked in a determined breath. No. No matter what the provocation, the luxury of escaping her fate with the arrogant King was simply not an option.

'But I don't want to call off the wedding,' she informed him quietly.

His eyes narrowed, but not before she'd seen the flicker of astonishment glinting in their pewter depths—as though someone disagreeing with him was something he wasn't used to. Zabrina could almost see the cogs of his brain whirling, as if he was trying to decide the best approach to take to kill off her rebellion, before it had a chance to grow.

'I'm sorry to disappoint you, Princess, but that's what's going to happen.'

'No. I think you misunderstand me, Roman. I am not disappointed. This is a decision I have made using my head, not my heart. This has nothing to do with emotion, because emotion has no place in this marriage of ours. It never did. I never particularly wanted it, if the truth were known, but I was willing to accept my fate.'

'Do you realise how much you insult me?' he breathed.

'It was not said with the purpose of insulting you. I said it because it was true. But the past is irrelevant.' She drew in a deep breath. 'The union must still take place. It has long been agreed. My country will benefit. Yours, too. Aren't you forgetting how much you desire that piece of land?'

'And aren't you forgetting something?' he snapped. 'Something less pragmatic than matters of finance and territory? It was always intended that my future queen should be—'

'Pure?' she interjected sarcastically. 'So you keep saying. Maybe it was and maybe I should be a lot more offended than I actually am that you don't believe I was. But I find I'm not offended at all—which I can only put down to the fact that I set the bar very low when it comes to my expectations concerning men!'

'Your negative opinions about men do not interest me. And I don't think you're hearing me properly, Zabrina. You are not what I consider to be a suitable partner and I do not want you as my wife.'

'And you're not hearing *me*,' she countered fiercely. 'You said yourself that my virginity was the unwritten clause in our wedding contract, and anyone who knows even a little bit of law realises that an unwritten clause means nothing!'

His eyes hardened. 'So you wish to force me to marry you? Is that what you really want? A man you have hounded to the altar? And all because your ego can't take perceived rejection.'

'It has nothing to do with my ego and everything to do with securing a prosperous future for my country!'

'And then what?' he demanded. 'Being with someone who doesn't want you is hardly a recipe for life-long contentment, is it?'

For a moment Zabrina was perplexed by his words—because surely he wasn't foolish enough to believe in fairy tales like *life-long contentment*. A relationship of polite civility and tolerance was the best that could be hoped for, because that was how these things worked. A royal marriage was about what the couple *represented* rather than the relationship which existed between them. She had even known she would be expected to turn a blind eye to his behaviour—to the liaisons with other women he would undoubtedly have—and she had been prepared to do that, because that had always been the case for the wives of kings.

She looked at him and thought about his words. 'But in some ways you *do* want me,' she said slowly.

'I'm not talking about sex!' he snapped.

'But isn't that also important? I mean, is what happened between us just then usual?'

'No, it isn't *usual*,' he said. 'You must know that.'

Zabrina nodded. She'd thought that to be the case. Perhaps in a different situation she might have been pleased by his acknowledgement of the powerful chemistry which existed between them, were his words not tinged with such obvious bitterness. And, of course, accusation. That subtle jibe about her supposed sexual experience hadn't escaped her. But she had lived a life where unfairness was something you just learned to live with and there was no reason why this should be any different.

'So why not just go through with it? It's not ideal, I know. But understand this, Roman. I've spent years preparing for my fate and if I hadn't, I might have lived my life very differently. I don't want to go back to Albastase as the Jilted Princess, and when you think about it you'll have to go to all the trouble of finding another bride who can provide you with an heir—that all-important means to securing and continuing your line of inheritance. Someone else who might just happen not to pass your exacting vetting process.'

There was silence for a moment. 'You mean you wish to bear my children?' he questioned slowly.

It had always been a given that she would do so and deep down Zabrina had always longed for children of her own. She thought of the fierce love she felt for her sisters and brother and how much she was going to miss them. Producing a family was an essential part of an arranged royal marriage, when you stopped to think about it, and yet it wasn't the kind of thing you spoke about in polite society. Yet as Roman asked the question, Zabrina felt a surge of something which felt like hope. Something which warmed and stirred her heart in a way she hadn't expected, but she kept her expression deadpan, because she suspected that somehow it would be more appropriate. That passion or eagerness might scare him.

'That has always been part of the deal, hasn't it?' she questioned quietly. 'We could make this marriage work, if we wanted it to. We don't seem to have a problem with communication and maybe that could work in our favour. We don't shy away from discussing things other people might find difficult. And neither of us believe in love, only duty. We have no foolish illusions, do we, Roman? No secret dreams ripe to be shattered. So, if you were to agree, we could continue on this train to the palace at Petrogoria and I could prepare for my life as your queen, as planned.'

There was a long pause before he spoke. 'Just like that?'

'Why not?'

His eyes narrowed, the silver gaze slicing through her like a blade. 'You've got it all worked out, haven't you, Princess?'

She wished he wouldn't use her title in that mocking way, because she liked it. She liked it more than she should. 'Let's just say I'm making the best of a bad situation.'

'And if I refuse? What then?'

His voice was silky but the note underpinning it was anything but. Zabrina imagined that tone might have intimidated many people, but it wasn't going to intimidate her. She shrugged, hearing the rhymical sound of the train as it thundered through the darkness towards Petrogoria. If she had been somebody else she might have threatened to go to the newspapers, because imagine all the money the press would pay for a juicy scoop like this—a respectable king pretending to be someone else and seducing the virgin princess! But she wouldn't do that—and not just because such a disclosure would drag both their names and their reputations through the mud. No. There were some things she would push for and some things she realised were pointless, because on an instinctive level she recognised that a man like Roman the Conqueror would never give in to something like blackmail.

'I don't think you will refuse,' she said, her gaze very steady. 'Because I think you need this marriage as much as I do.'

CHAPTER SEVEN

THERE WERE FLOWERS EVERYWHERE. Bright flowers which filled the air with their heady scent. Roses and gerbera. Delphinium and lilac. Pink and blue and red and orange and every conceivable shade in between. Swathes of them festooned the railway station at Rosumunte and yet more were waved by the packed crowds lining the roads to the palace. Petals were thrown towards their open-topped car and most fluttered to the ground but some were captured by the inert wipers and lay against the car's windscreen, where already they were beginning to wilt in the warm sunshine.

And there were so many *people*. In the pale blue silk dress which had been specially chosen for this occasion, Zabrina sat bolt upright beside the King, who was raising his hand to his adoring subjects, and she forced herself to follow suit. 'Gosh,' she breathed, her heart missing yet another beat. 'This is…'

He turned to her, his face shadowed and enigmatic despite the bright sunshine. 'What?'

She swallowed but somehow turned the movement into a small smile, the sort of smile her new subjects would expect to see, because she wasn't supposed to be inside her own head, thinking about the man whose thigh was so tantalisingly close to hers. She was supposed to be thinking about other things. Like that sweet little girl by the roadside, who was waving like crazy in her direction. Zabrina lifted her fingers in response and the child's smile widened.

But it wasn't easy to rid her thoughts of the devastatingly handsome King, because it took some getting used to—seeing him in uniform when before she'd only ever seen him in billowing shirt, trousers and long boots. And naked, of course. She mustn't forget that. But the Petrogorian army uniform was dark and formal and did incredible things for his already impressive physique. It emphasised the hard, honed body, while the peaked cap drew attention to the shadowed jut of his jaw and the proud posture which made his shoulders look so broad. Zabrina cleared her throat. 'It's massive,' she breathed. 'I wasn't expecting all these people to turn out to greet me.'

'You are their future Queen. Of course they wish to welcome you.'

'I know, and I appreciate that. It's just that you can be aware of something intellectually, but, when it happens, it doesn't feel how you thought it would feel.'

'And how does it make you feel? Nervous?'

She folded her hands together in her lap, terrified he would notice the tell-tale dampness of her palms, because hadn't she fought for this? To be Roman's future queen and to bear his children? In which case it would be inappropriate to showcase a quivering mass of uncertainties which seemed to have come at her out of nowhere. 'I was told many years ago that nerves have no place in the life of a princess.'

'And did you believe everything you were told, Zabrina?'

'I suppose I did,' she said carefully, resolutely ignoring the trace of mockery in his voice. 'Doesn't every child put their faith in the adults who form their view of the world?'

His laugh was unexpectedly bitter and the lines around his mouth became deep and tense. 'Not necessarily. Not if they've discovered such an exercise to be futile.'

'Is that what happened to you?'

'I don't dwell on the past, Zabrina. It's pointless.'

She wanted to argue that the past informed the present and to tell him that she needed to get to know him better, but something told her now was not the time and her immediate concerns were of a far more practical nature. Soon they would arrive at the palace and, if her own father's exalted position was anything to go by, the King would quickly be surrounded and swept away by a cohort of aides and equerries. And she would be on her own. Alone in a place where she knew absolutely no one.

Except him.

She moistened her lips with the tip of her tongue. 'So what happens when we reach the palace? What's the set-up there?'

He shrugged. 'The set-up will be exactly as was always planned. You will have your own staff. A private secretary with their own office, plus various ladies-in-waiting who will provide you with anything you need. You will obviously wish to explore as much of Petrogoria as is possible in the run-up to the marriage and to acquaint yourself with your new country and its people. Some of these visits we will do together, some you will perform solo and, once we are married, we will tour nearby Greece.'

She touched one of the waxy blooms of the lily-of-the-valley bouquet she had been presented with on embarkation and fixed her gaze on his. 'I was told that it would be possible for my horse to be brought here. And before you start telling me that you have the finest stable of horses in the world—it's not the same as having a mount you've owned ever since he was a young foal.'

'Of course you can have your horse here. I will set the process in motion,' he said, his eyes narrowing, as if he had picked up some of her apprehension. 'The aim is to make you feel at home, Zabrina, not alienate you, and all efforts have been made to do this.

Your suite of rooms is in the southern end of the palace, where the outlook is particularly fine. I am sure you've heard about the fabled gardens here, which have inspired some of the nation's finest poets and—'

'Of course I have,' she interjected quickly, because he was the last person she could imagine enjoying poetry and just the thought of that was more than a little distracting. 'But what about you?'

'Perhaps you could be a little more specific, Princess.' His grey eyes gleamed with yet more mockery. 'What *about* me?'

'Is your…?' A lump seemed to have inconveniently lodged itself in her throat, making her next words come out as a thready whisper. 'Is your own section of the palace nearby?'

'Why, is that what you were hoping for?'

'Of course not,' she said crossly, but her burning cheeks ran the risk of making her words seem like a sham.

'I have decided that there will be no resumption of intimacy until we take our vows, as tradition demands. So I'm afraid you will just have to survive on the memory of how good it can be, Princess.'

'Does anyone know?' she questioned, in a low voice.

'You mean, are my staff aware that we've already had sex?'

'Keep your voice down!' she hissed. 'How…how are you going to explain the fact that you were even *on* my train when it arrived this morning, when I was supposed to meet you for the first time at the station? I could tell the crowds were surprised when they saw you jumping off in front of me and then lifting me down.' She raised her hand to wave to the crowds, her serene smile belying the rapid thunder of her heart. 'A completely over-the-top response, in my opinion.'

Roman expelled a reluctant sigh as the sunlight splashed pale gold streaks over her dark hair, because the reworking of the original plan had given him cause for concern. He had considered having the train make an unscheduled stop just outside the capital, and for one of his grooms to have a horse saddled and ready for him to ride to 'meet' the Princess for the first time. But the thought of any more subterfuge had been wearisome and he couldn't guarantee how Zabrina would react to such a suggestion—negatively, he suspected. And besides, he was the King. If he occasionally broke the rules, so what?

'I've already spoken to my aides and given them a story.'

'A *story*?'

'Don't look so shocked, Princess. Isn't that what everyone does?' He saw an old woman lay her hand across her heart as he passed by and he gave a courteous nod of acknowledgement. 'Reality is just an interpretation of facts,' he continued smoothly. 'And no two people ever see things the same way. I told them I was determined to protect my future bride and the most effective way of ensuring that was to guard her myself.'

'Right. Because the real facts—the true facts— that you were secretly doing a character assassination of me, wouldn't play out very sympathetically for you, would they, Roman?'

'Possibly not,' he mused. A flurry of rose petals drifted into the car and as one of them lodged itself beneath a pearl clip which gleamed in her hair, Roman had the strongest desire to smooth it away with his finger. But he didn't. He didn't trust himself to touch her again. At least, not yet. And certainly not in public, where his every action would be forensically scrutinised. What if some clever camera lens managed to capture his gnawing frustration at the way control seemed to be slipping away from him whenever he was around her?

Because none of this was turning out as he'd expected. He had thought, after deciding to go ahead with the marriage, that they might spend the remainder of the night on the train, blissfully exploring each other's bodies. There had certainly been plenty of sexual tension fizzing between them, after she'd given him all the reasons why they *shouldn't* call off the union. In a way, he had almost admired her dogged determination to get her own way. It had certainly turned him on. And while he was aware that sexual propriety would have to be observed once they reached the palace and they wouldn't be intimate again until their wedding night—surely that was even more reason to have capitalised on the strange circumstances which had led to that first delicious encounter. Silviana the servant could have been dismissed for the night and he could have locked the carriage door and let bliss take over.

But it had seemed that Zabrina had other ideas.

In fact, he had conducted the remainder of the journey standing to attention in the rattling corridor of the train, right outside her salon.

'If you're so determined to pretend to be a body-guard, then maybe you'd better start acting like one!' she had hissed, before slamming the door in his face—something which had never happened to him, not in all his thirty-three years.

Outside his stint in the Petrogorian army or those heart-knotting times after his mother had deserted him, it had been the longest night of his life—not helped by the thought of Zabrina lying in bed only a few metres away. At the beginning of his long shift, thinking about her and what they had done together had been a welcome distraction—until it had become a self-induced form of torture. He had found himself wondering whether she slept naked. He had begun picturing her tiny frame and the slender curves which had wrapped themselves around him so accommo-datingly, and his body had stiffened with such a hard jerk of desire that a passing guard had looked at him with concern and asked if he was okay.

Of course he hadn't been okay! He had been frustrated in more ways than one—furious at having been wrong-footed by the foxy Princess. A part of him still was...

'And do you still think it was a good idea?' she questioned suddenly, her soft voice breaking into the muddle of his thoughts. 'To pretend to be someone you weren't, just to find out what I was really like?'

He looked at her. It would have been easy to say no, that he regretted all the subterfuge and deceit, and surely that would dissolve some of the strain which had tightened her features. But a defining—and possibly redeeming—feature of their relationship had emerged during the short time they had known one another. She had said so herself. They had no illusions of love. No foolish dreams to shatter. Couldn't total honesty elevate this arranged marriage into something which didn't need hollow and placatory words to survive?

'Perhaps the manner of execution wasn't ideal,' he mused. 'But if you're asking whether I regret having got to know you in that way, then the answer would have to be no. If we had been introduced in the traditional way, then all kinds of barriers would have been erected. We would have made polite small talk and been forced to endure a stilted courtship. And yes, it is going to be something of a farce and frustration to deny ourselves physical satisfaction in the run-up to the wedding, but it will certainly hone our mutual desire.' He turned and slanted her a complicit smile. 'Which is presumably why you kicked me out of the carriage last night.'

'I did that because I didn't trust myself not to kick you literally!'

He could feel the flicker of a smile tugging at the edges of his lips. 'If you want me to be perfectly frank, it was something of a relief to discover you were sexually experienced.'

'It was?' she verified, her voice growing a little faint.

'Undoubtedly.' He turned and waved to someone in the crowd who was calling out his name. 'To be honest, virgins are hard work.'

'Hard work?' she echoed dully. 'In what way?'

He shook his head. 'It doesn't matter.'

'Oh, I think it does.'

'You don't want to know.'

'Oh, but that's where you're wrong, Roman. I do. I thought we were going to be frank with one another. I don't want you to spare my feelings.'

He shrugged. 'If you want the truth, virgins need constant reassurance. They don't seem to realise that if you're constantly asking a man whether or not he likes it and whether or not you're doing it properly, it's a bit of a turn-off.'

'I see.' She pressed her lips together in what he was now coming to recognise was one of her determined smiles. 'Well, I'm glad we've got that out of the way! Thanks very much for the enlightenment.'

Roman's eyes narrowed. In many ways she surprised him as well as amused him, but there was something about her which was... He shook his head, unable to define what it was he was feeling and that did not sit comfortably with him. And surely it was simpler to push such feelings aside… He cleared his throat. 'If you look straight ahead,' he said unevenly, 'you'll get your first view of the palace, with the Liliachiun mountains behind.'

The iconic towers of the Petrogorian palace soared into view, but Zabrina could barely focus on the pale-hued magnificence of the ancient building ahead, so great was her anger towards the man by her side. He was…*unbearable*. He was the most unspeakably arrogant man it had ever been her misfortune to meet and if she was now committed to spending the rest of her life with him, she had only herself to blame.

So how come she still fancied him like crazy, even though some of the things he came out with made her want to scream with rage?

His damning assessment of virgins and their *constant need for reassurance* had been unbelievable! Was that how he regarded everyone who came into his orbit? In terms of how they impacted on him? Why, he'd made it sound as if he found some women boring even while he was actually having sex with them! Her heart missed a beat as an annoying flash of jealousy shot through her like a dark flame at the thought of him being intimate with another woman, but, once it had passed, her overriding emotion was one of relief. Thank heavens she hadn't asked him if she was pleasing him! Or if she was 'doing it right'.

But it hadn't been like that, she remembered. There had been no sense of inequality when they had both lain naked on that sofa. It hadn't felt as if he was the super-experienced one—which he clearly was—while she didn't have a clue, because she had never done it before. Because everything which had happened seemed to have happened so naturally. As if, on a physical level at least, they *knew* one another.

She shook her head a little because thoughts like that were dangerous. Fanciful. If she wasn't careful, she would start believing her own stupid fairy-tale version of what had happened. And Roman had tacitly warned her not to do that. He'd said that reality was just a personal interpretation of facts. So she'd better be careful not to misinterpret them.

Surreptitiously, she wiped her palms over the skirt of her silk dress and looked ahead. She could see even more crowds gathered outside the gilded gates of the palace and a huge cheer went up as the open-topped car began to make its stately progress up the wide, tree-lined boulevard.

'Do you like it?' Roman was saying. 'Your new home?'

Zabrina's eyes narrowed as they grew closer. She had seen pictures of the palace, of course she had, for it was widely acknowledged to be one of the finest examples of imperial architecture to be found anywhere in the world. The walls were the colour of rich cream, the conical towers rose-gold. Arched windows were edged with pale stone and a pair of intricately carved columns stood on either side of the vast main doors. In the distance she could see a glimpse of the famous gardens and parkland and, beyond that, the soaring splendour of the Liliachiun mountains.

'It's…beautiful,' she said truthfully, but then almost regretted the sincerity of her words because they had caused Roman to smile with genuine pleasure, and she was ill prepared for the impact of that smile. Did he realise it was like the sun coming out from behind a thunder-dark cloud? He must do. Someone in the past must have told him that when he smiled like that it was like discovering something you'd never realised existed. As if you'd just looked up into the sky and noticed that a second sun had suddenly made an unexpected appearance.

And then he went and spoiled it.

'So you think you will be able to tolerate your position here?' he questioned coolly. 'As the wealthiest consort on the planet, with untold riches at your disposal.'

'How greedy you make me sound,' she reflected, but the stupid thing was that it hurt. She didn't want it to be all about money. She wanted it to be about feelings.

But his steely gaze was completely lacking in emotion. 'Not greedy, Zabrina,' he said calmly. 'Just practical. We're both going into this marriage because of what we stand to gain. And I think it's wise to acknowledge that, don't you? I read the prenuptial contract thoroughly before signing. I saw the clause your lawyer insisted on inserting—that you would be guaranteed a private income of your own.'

His black brows were raised in arrogant query as if demanding an explanation, but Zabrina was damned if she was going to give him one. She had her reasons for wanting that money, but she wasn't ready to share them with him and maybe she never would be. He probably wouldn't believe her anyway. And wasn't there something a bit sad about someone who insisted on pointing out what a do-gooder they were? She didn't trust him, he didn't trust her, so maybe they should just leave it at that.

She shrugged. 'And I noticed your lawyer inserted a rider to that clause, saying that I would only get the money for as long as the marriage lasted.'

'Of course he did. Otherwise there would be no incentive for you to make the marriage work, would there? You could just take the money and run.'

He said something harsh beneath his breath, and Zabrina frowned.

'Did you just say…"*just like my mother*"?' she asked slowly.

She spoke without thinking and must have hit a raw nerve because a flash of something dark ravaged the carved beauty of his face. It was as if he'd put on a savage mask which made him almost unrecognisable, but it was gone in an instant, his features shuttered and emotionless again—as if he was all too aware that the prying lenses of the cameras were trained on them.

'I had forgotten that you spoke fluent Petrogorian,' he bit out. 'Perhaps I would do well to guard my tongue in future. But even so, do you consider this is an appropriate time to ambush me with such questions?'

Zabrina was aware that she had either hurt or angered him but she hadn't meant to do either. It hadn't been intended as a point-scoring exercise, or a desire to catch him off-guard—she'd just wanted to find out more about the man she was to marry.

'Roman—'

'Let's just concentrate on what we're supposed to be doing, shall we?' he interrupted, his lips barely moving as he edged out the words—presumably to foil any would-be lip-readers. 'And smile. No, a *big* smile, Princess. Act like you really mean it. We're here.'

The powerful car drew to a halt in front of the applauding palace staff and Zabrina glanced up to see figures clustered at upstairs windows high above, capturing the image on their cell-phones. Roman leapt from the car and opened her car door himself and as he held out his hand to help her down, Zabrina was aware of two things. Firstly, that the brief touch of his fingers was enough to send soft shivers of desire rippling down her spine, making her wish he would lift them to his lips and kiss them. But he didn't.

Because the second thing she noticed—and this was the one which stayed with her for the rest of the day—was that the grey eyes which were turned in her direction were as empty and as cold as ice.

CHAPTER EIGHT

SOFT SUNLIGHT FLICKERED over the profuse spill of roses, bathing the famous gardens in a rich golden glow as Zabrina stared out of the vast windows.

But no matter how hard she tried to concentrate on the beauty outside, or on the small dish of fruit on the table in front of her, it was difficult to focus on anything other than the devastatingly handsome man who was seated opposite. The morning light was glinting on his cropped dark hair, making her realise how much it had grown, and his snowy white shirt emphasised the muscular width of his shoulders.

Suddenly he pushed his empty coffee cup away and leaned back in his chair to study her. Was he aware she'd been watching him with a hungry desire which wouldn't seem to go away? And did that fill him with a sense of triumph—and power?

'Today's the big day, isn't it?' he said.

Zabrina gazed at him blankly. The only 'big day' which seemed to be on everyone's lips wasn't for another three weeks—unless somebody had brought the wedding forward and not bothered to tell the bride. She hoped not, because there were still what looked like five million seed pearls to sew onto her traditional Petrogorian wedding dress and sequins which needed to be scattered all over her tulle veil. She picked up her silver spoon, still trying to get used to the enormous emerald and diamond engagement ring which felt too heavy for her finger. 'Big day?' she repeated.

'Your horse,' he said. 'What time does it arrive?'

'He. The horse is a he, not an it,' Zabrina corrected, watching as a servant silently moved forward to refill the King's cup with inky-black coffee. 'And his name is Midas.'

'Ah!' He picked up a sugar cube. 'Named after the king who wished for an excess of gold and almost ruined his life in the process?'

'That's the one.'

He lifted his dark brows in arrogant query. 'Perhaps there is an allegory in that story for us, Zabrina.'

'Let's hope not,' she said darkly.

A brief smile curved the edges of his lips as he dropped the sugar into the cup and began to stir and Zabrina found herself mesmerised by the circular movement of his fingers, wondering how he could make such a simple action look so insanely sexy. But then, he made just about everything he did look sexy. Was that deliberate? Was he taunting her? Reminding her of that heart-punching intimacy they'd shared on the Petrogoria-bound train, which was now being put on hold until they were married?

Stop it, she thought. *Just stop it. You are supposed to be having a polite breakfast conversation about the day ahead.*

The kind of measured diary conversation they'd been having every morning since she'd arrived in Petrogoria last week. This was the public face of their formal engagement, as opposed to the private anxieties which plagued her every night when she was alone in bed.

Over coffee, fruit and eggs over easy—for him— they would go through the various royal duties which had been mapped out for them by their private offices—some together and some apart. Solo duties she welcomed. In many ways, it was less distracting when Roman wasn't by her side distracting her with his powerful presence.

Hadn't she thought—hoped—that he would go back on his determination for their nights to be spent separately? But she had been wrong. He hadn't and now she had started to wonder if his reluctance to touch her meant he was having second thoughts about the wedding. But rejection was something she wouldn't countenance—not now—and so she threw herself into her new charities with fervour, hoping that her engagements would make her fit in and feel easier about her place here.

Because Roman had been right. Or rather, Roman when he had been masquerading as Constantin and answering her questions with an alluring frankness, leaving her wondering which of them was the real man. The understanding and passionate bodyguard, or the cold, disciplined king?

It didn't matter.

The fact remained that the royal palace of Petrogoria *was* intimidating, just as he'd warned her.

For a start it was big. Way bigger than she'd imagined and everything was on a much larger scale than what she was used to. It made her childhood home seem like a matchbox lined up next to a shoebox. And it wasn't just the size—it was all the contents. There was more of *everything*. More Old Master paintings, more ancient books and precious artefacts. The scaled-up fountains sprayed bigger and more impressive plumes of water and the corridors seemed endless. And these weren't the familiar corridors of home—the ones which she'd run along and explored and hidden in, from when she'd first learned to walk. These were impossibly wide marble passageways, lined by inscrutable servants who bowed or curtseyed whenever she passed them. Here there were no friendly cooks or grooms who'd known her since babyhood and who had treated her with a slightly modified version of informality, which she'd always found comforting.

Roman had described it as home.

It just didn't feel like *her* home.

Life here was like being part of a beautifully choreographed dance—with the King positioned at its glittering centre. Everything revolved around him. Sometimes Zabrina felt like a satellite to his blazing sun—as if she were an insignificant and very distant star. Each day they took their meals together in different dining rooms, all of them exquisite. They ate breakfast overlooking the fabled rose gardens and lunch was taken in a huge windowed chamber, decorated in a dizzying spectrum of blues. Dinner was served either in the supposedly more low-key Rose Room—which wasn't low-key at all—or, if they had company, in the highly ornate Golden Dining Room. Because if people were coming to eat in a palace as famous as this one, they liked to really feel they'd had the whole palace 'experience'.

After dinner she and Roman might have a nightcap—rare—before retiring to their separate suites, though she gathered from remarks which Silviana had made that the King often worked in his study until the early hours of the morning. Whatever he did, it didn't involve her. In fact, none of his life did. Not physically, at least. Amid the careful carving out of her role as his future queen and the increasingly frenetic arrangements for the wedding, there had been no rerun of that heady sensual episode on the train.

The King of Petrogoria had not laid a finger on her since she'd walked over the threshold of his glittering golden palace.

Had she thought it might be different?

Yes, of course she had.

Had she offended him hugely by kicking him out
of her carriage that night, when it had been obvious
that—after all the dust had settled—he had wanted
to stay and carry on with more of what they'd been
doing? Probably. She had felt so strong and so sure of
herself at the time. She'd been infused with a powerful sense of self brought about by that magical sexual
encounter and had felt no qualms about castigating
him for his deception, and for refusing to believe that
he was her first lover.

Yet the annoying thing was that her show of de-
fiance seemed to have backfired on her—because
he had taken her at her word, quite literally! And by
keeping his physical distance, he had managed to
fill her with a lingering sense of uncertainty. The
brief and heady authority she had felt when he had
been in her arms had shifted, and now *he* was the
one who seemed to possess all the power. She wondered if she had wounded his pride and ego in such
a way that he now found the thought of touching her
unpalatable. Should she ask him?

*Roman, don't you find me sexually attractive any
more?*

Roman, don't you want to take me to bed?

No. Because deep down she knew the answer to
that, no matter how insecure she sometimes felt. It
was made plain by the smoky hunger which flared
in his eyes whenever she inadvertently caught him
watching her, before quickly composing his handsome face into its more habitual impassive mask. He

still wanted her, all right. That mutual desire showed no sign of abating. Predictably and potently, it fizzed between them whenever they were in the same room together. Like a flame, she thought, with equal longing and despair—bright and vital—yet tantalisingly ephemeral.

His grey gaze was fixed on her questioningly. 'So is he gold?'

'Who?' She looked at him in confusion, trying to gather together the scramble of her thoughts. 'Oh, you mean Midas?'

He made no attempt to hide his sardonic smile. 'Isn't that what we've just been talking about?'

She flushed, wondering if he had any idea what had been preoccupying her. She hoped not. Though what did she know? Probably any woman who found herself alone with him spent the majority of their time fantasising about what he was like in bed. It was almost a pity that she had actually experienced it—because didn't that make it harder to shift the tantalising images from her head?

She cleared her throat and forced herself to concentrate on her beloved horse. 'No, he's not really golden. More of a bay. An Akhal Teke, actually. But when I first got him it was my birthday and I was taken down to the stables early in the morning and there he was, with the sunshine glinting off his coat like metal—and he looked…well, he looked magical really. Like a living golden statue.' She paused, the iced mango in her bowl forgotten as an unexpected wave of nostalgia washed over her and she looked at him rather sheepishly, surprised by the narrowed interest in his grey eyes. 'I don't know what made me tell you that.'

But she did know. It was just a long time since she'd allowed herself to think about it.

It had been one of those unusual periods of her upbringing when an air of something like calm had settled over the palace, mostly because her father had returned into the bosom of his family after his latest affair. After one of these interludes, her mother's overriding reaction would always be one of profound relief that everything could be 'normal' again. Often, this would provide the ideal opportunity for the palace to release a photo depicting happy family life. It was also one of the reasons why her father would overcompensate—materially, at least—and overspend even more than usual. Thus, Zabrina had been gifted a beautiful and very expensive horse with a scarlet ribbon tied around his neck and the cake they had all eaten later for her birthday tea had been ridiculously big.

The memory of that monstrous gateau made her feel a little nauseous and she pushed her half-eaten dish of mango away, forcing herself to change the subject. But maybe she should capitalise on the fact that Roman seemed to have let his guard down and this was the most relaxed he'd been. There were a million questions she wanted to ask him but instinct told her that she needed to tread carefully. Maybe he was like a prized thoroughbred, who needed careful handling. 'Can I ask you something, Roman?'

Instantly, his eyes narrowed with caution. 'You can ask. I won't guarantee that I'll answer.'

She wondered if he had been a lawyer in a previous life. 'Are you planning to do anything with the Marengo Forest after our wedding?'

Roman sat back in his chair as he stared into the long-lashed beauty of her green eyes. She could be quite…unexpected, he conceded. He had imagined her mind to be flapping with those tiresome thoughts women so often entertained and had been anticipating her demanding to know how he 'felt' about her. And that was the last thing he wanted to answer. Because the bizarre truth of that was he didn't really know and there was no way he wanted Zabrina to realise that.

She seemed such a contradiction. Sometimes seasoned, sometimes innocent, sometimes spoiled and at others sweetly thoughtful. Her complexity intrigued him and he had no wish to be intrigued, because that wasn't what this union was supposed to be about. She unsettled him and he didn't like being unsettled by a woman. Hadn't he vowed that was never going to happen to him again? That no woman should have any kind of power over his thoughts and his feelings?

That was one of the reasons why he hadn't touched her since he'd brought her to his palace. Why he hadn't given into the silken tug of desire even though every time he saw her he grew exquisitely hard. He swallowed. Before her arrival, she had been allotted a separate suite at the opposite end of the vast palace complex. At the time he had accepted there would be no sex before marriage because the Princess was a virgin and tradition demanded it. And even though her subsequent behaviour had meant there was no reason for such a restriction, he saw no reason to change the existing plan, because he could see a definite advantage to denial—no matter how frustrating he might find it.

Because hadn't Zabrina of Albastase smashed down all his carefully erected defences that night? Hadn't he found himself unable to resist her in a way which had been mind-blowingly unique? His mouth hardened. She had made him lose control in a way which was alien to him, transforming him into a man he didn't recognise, or particularly respect. In her arms he had felt as if he had died and gone to heaven and it had been terrifying and delicious. But he realised it had put her firmly in the driving seat and he wanted to shift the balance of power back in his favour. And *that* was why he continued to distance himself from his future bride, no matter how great the cost to his equilibrium.

She wanted him. Of course she did. Every woman had always wanted him, ever since he'd reached puberty. But what he felt for her was right off the scale. It was as though provocative and carnal invitation thrummed from every pore of her delicious body.

At times it became almost too much to bear and he was tempted to throw caution to the winds and take her in his arms. His fantasy involved either the slowest removal of lingerie in the history of the world, or ripping off her panties and plunging deep into her syrupy heat as her little cries of encouragement urged him on.

But he wasn't going to do that. He was going to make her wait, even if he half tortured himself with frustration in the process. He would demonstrate icy control and defer delight until the appropriate time and that would be an invaluable lesson in self-denial. Zabrina would come to him on their wedding night, humbled by his restraint and eager to taste pleasure once again. Because delay heightened hunger.

His mouth twisted.

Or so he'd heard.

He looked at the gleam of wavy dark hair which fell so abundantly over her shoulders. At the green silk dress which matched her eyes and clung so enticingly to the small and perfect breasts. He'd thought about those breasts a lot recently, especially at night when he'd been lying in his lonely bed, sleeplessly staring as the shifting moon painted the walls silver. Just as he'd thought about her strong, slim thighs and the way his head had fitted so perfectly between them.

'Of course I'm planning to *do* something with the Marengo Forest,' he said, reluctantly dragging his thoughts back to the present, knowing he had no one but himself to blame for the hard throb of his erection. He cleared his throat. 'Its return has been in my sights for a long time and I have big plans for it.'

She looked up from where she had begun to pleat her napkin with those tanned fingers which had worked such magic on his shuddering flesh. 'You do?'

He frowned. 'Why else do you think I should go to so much trouble to acquire it? Why I'm prepared to pay such a monumental amount of money for it, in the form of your dowry?'

'I hope you think I'm worth it.'

He saw her cheeks colour and momentarily felt a little bad as she made the sardonic comment, but only for a moment. Hadn't they both agreed to be pragmatic about the situation? 'It's a deal, Zabrina,' he said simply. 'Remember? And this is not just about territory—about me having some hypothetical need to return the Petrogorian flag to its rightful place. I want to build an airport nearby—it's a pristine, natural wilderness which is ripe for sympathetic eco-tourism.'

'Oh.' Her fingers stilled on the napkin, the white linen folds making her skin look like softest gold. 'Oh, I see.'

'So what makes you appear so crestfallen?' he enquired idly. 'The price I'm paying for that piece of land is more than you could have ever hoped of achieving, if you'd sold it on the open market. Even you must realise that.'

'Yes, of course I do. It's not that.'

'What, then?'

'It doesn't matter.' She shook her head. 'It won't be of any possible interest to you.'

'Why don't you let me be the judge of that?' He took a sip of coffee. 'I'm interested to know what's making you bite your lip as if you have all the cares of the world on your shoulders.'

Imprisoned in the grey spotlight of his narrowed eyes, Zabrina hesitated. Should she tell him what she'd been thinking? This was to be nothing but a marriage of 'convenience', which presumably meant they could keep things on a very superficial level. But what was the point of keeping everything buttoned up inside her? Wasn't one of the benefits of a live-in relationship supposed to be that you were at liberty to confide in your partner? And surely it would be good to talk to someone who might actually *listen*, rather than her mother—on whose deaf ears Zabrina's concerns had always fallen, so that she'd given up expressing her fears a long time ago.

'If you must know, I admire your ambitious plans about a region which has lain neglected for so long…'

'But? I suspect there's a "but" coming?'

'I guess I'm also slightly frustrated that my country didn't think of doing it first.'

'Either nobody considered it, or they didn't have the wherewithal to carry it out. Presumably the latter.' He looked at her with a steady gaze. 'It usually boils down to hard finance, Zabrina.'

'I know it does.' She puffed out an unsteady breath. 'I suppose I'm also concerned about the amount of money you're paying for the land. And for me,' she finished drily.

He raised his eyebrows. 'You don't think it's enough?'

She gave a short laugh. 'Nobody in the world could think that. It's an extremely generous amount of money. I'm more worried about what's going to happen to it when it lands in my father's bank account.'

'He could spend it wisely. Make sure it's ploughed back into the country.' He gave a shrug. 'You know. Invest in some new infrastructure.'

Zabrina could feel her cheeks colour as she wondered whether it might be wise to close the subject down. Anyone who had been to Albastase knew it was getting very frayed around the edges, but few people knew just how inept the King was at managing finances. Sometimes she wished this money had been transferred directly to the government, bypassing the royal coffers, giving him little opportunity to fritter it away—but she could hardly denounce her own father.

'I hope so.'

'You don't sound very convinced.'

She had obviously failed to inject a tone of enthusiasm into her voice but Roman's perception surprised her. She hadn't thought of him as a student of nuance. Just as she hadn't expected him to continue to regard her with what looked like genuine interest.

And somehow she started telling him about it. Stuff which she never talked about with her family, because there had been no point. Her mother could not or would not act, her sisters were too young and uninterested and her brother... Zabrina swallowed. Her brother was already having difficulty coming to terms with the fact that one day he would be King and she didn't want to be the one to add to those concerns. They had been like the family of someone with an unacknowledged drinking problem...as if by ignoring it, the problem would somehow go away.

'My father can sometimes be...extravagant.'

'That is surely one of the perks of being a king.'

Her jaw worked and somehow all her fears about leaving everyone back home to fend for themselves came tumbling out. 'No. This is more than having a garage full of fancy cars, or a fleet of racehorses which he keeps overseas.'

'I'm glad about that,' he said wryly. 'Or I might find myself the subject of your obvious disapproval.'

She shook her head slightly impatiently. 'It's more than extravagance. He's surrounded by a coterie of stupid advisors and the trouble is that he listens to them. They keep getting him to invest in their friends' supposedly amazing business schemes, only they never quite work out the way they're supposed to and he gets his fingers burned. Every time.'

'Then one has to ask the question as to why he

keeps doing it,' said Roman coolly. 'Don't they say that the definition of madness is to keep repeating the same mistake, over and over again?'

'Because he doesn't believe in his own fallibility and when it happens, he needs something to reassure him that he's as clever as he thinks he is,' said Zabrina quietly. 'Which is why, after every failure, he grabs at that guaranteed age-old ego boost so beloved of men.' And wasn't it crazy that she *still* felt a sense of guilt as she admitted the truth to the man she was soon to marry, as if she were wrong to criticise her own father. Yet in the midst of all these misgivings, it felt a huge relief to be able to confide in him like this.

'And you're worried because your country is gradually being run down?' Roman questioned.

'Of course I am. But I'm more worried that by the time my brother Alexandru inherits, there won't be anything left. He's a delicate young man,' she whispered. 'And super-sensitive. I'd hate for him to take on the burden of kingship if he was also saddled by an enormous debt!' she finished, her lips wobbling a little with the impact of expressing all that usually bottled-up emotion. She looked into the King's face but, as usual, its cool impassiveness gave nothing away.

Instead he raised his fingers and the servant brought him another cup of coffee, before Roman indicated he should leave—signalling that this breakfast might go on longer than anticipated. And that surprised Zabrina, because usually these meal times were strictly regulated and chaperoned—as if the man she was to marry couldn't bear to be alone in her company a second more than he needed to.

'I can understand that,' he said slowly. 'But now you've triggered my interest.'

'Oh?'

He lifted his gaze to hers. 'What *exactly* is the age-old ego boost your father always resorts to?'

She guessed they'd always needed to have this discussion, so why not now, even though it wasn't really the kind of thing she'd ever imagined discussing calmly over the muesli? Because Roman was a king and what she was about to talk about was what all kings did. It came with the territory and she was surprised he even needed to ask.

'Affairs,' she said simply. 'He has affairs.'

CHAPTER NINE

ROMAN STUDIED ZABRINA'S expression with a curiosity he didn't bother to hide, because something about the calm acceptance he read there surprised him. 'Explain,' he clipped out. 'About your father's affairs.'

She shrugged with studied carelessness, but he didn't miss the fleeting look of apprehension which crossed her eyes.

'They usually come about as a reaction to one of his disastrous business investments,' she began slowly. 'You see, he loses huge amounts of money and promises himself it will never happen again.' She stared at the pink roses in the vase at the centre of the table, before lifting her gaze to his again. 'But in the meantime he needs something to make him feel better—to take his mind off what he's done. And women can do that. They can fill that emotional hole—just like a drink or an unnecessary plate of food. And, of course, he's a king. So he can do what the hell he likes.'

'Isn't that a rather sweeping generalisation?'

She laughed. A sound he had heard only infrequently and usually he was forced to steel himself against its soft lure, but now it was edged with the hard ring of cynicism.

'I'm only basing my comments on experience, Roman.'

'Of observing your father, you mean?'

She shook her head. 'No, not just that. Don't forget my mother is a princess herself and she and her sisters all married monarchs and, according to her, they have all "strayed". I always thought that was a funny expression to use,' she added reflectively. 'It reminds me of a horse or a cow somehow managing to get out of its enclosure.'

He guessed that was supposed to be a joke but the brittle note in her voice suggested she wasn't as comfortable with the subject as she wanted him to think.

'So your mother just accepted this state of affairs, if you'll excuse the pun?'

She didn't laugh, just shrugged. 'In a way. She said it was easier to accept than to constantly rail against something she couldn't change. She told me that husbands always returned—eventually. Especially if there was a calm and non-accusatory welcome for them to come back to. And especially if there were children involved.'

He felt the chill of something dark. The indelible shadow of his childhood making itself known without warning. His heart clenched with pain but he was practised enough to be able to eject the thought and corresponding emotion as far from his mind as possible, and to continue to subject Zabrina to a steady stare instead. 'And what about wives?' he questioned softly. 'Do they also stray?'

Either she was genuinely shocked by his question or she was a superb actress, for her lips fell open and she frowned.

'Well, no. She never did.'

'Why not?'

'Because men are different.'

'In other ways than anatomically, you mean?' he challenged, disproportionately pleased to see the blush which made her cheeks colour so thoroughly.

She glared. 'That's not funny. It's a biological thing, or so my mother always said. I'm not saying that infidelity is necessarily a good idea—more that it's understandable. Nature's way of ensuring the human race continues, because men—'

'I get the idea, Zabrina. There's no need to spell it out,' he interrupted drily, taking a final sip of coffee before pushing his cup away. 'So will your extremely liberal views on fidelity impact on our own marriage?'

She paused. For effect, Roman suspected, more than anything else. Because surely she must have given this subject *some* consideration in the light of her own experience.

'This is a duty marriage,' she said at last. 'And I don't have any unrealistic expectations about that side of it. I know that men often get bored when they have been intimate with one woman for any length of time, and that they crave new excitement.'

'Who the hell told you *that*?'

'My mother. She's a very practical person.'

Roman thought these views cynical rather than practical, but he didn't say so. 'I see.'

'What's important to me is providing a secure base for the family we both hope to have.'

'Well, that's something, at least,' he said and maybe some of his own cynicism had become apparent because she shot him a quick and rather worried look.

'You do *want* a family?' she verified. 'I mean, I know we touched on it on the train—'

'We did a lot of touching on the train, Zabrina.'

'That's not funny.'

'No?'

'No.' Her voice was bitter. 'I wish I could forget that trip.'

'So do I,' he said, with more force than he had intended.

'All I ask…'

He could see her throat constricting and she appeared to be conducting a struggle to find the right words. 'Don't upset yourself,' he said, with a sudden wave of empathy which surprised him. 'We don't have to talk about this right now.'

'But we do. We need to get all these things out of the way. All I ask,' she continued stolidly, 'is that you're discreet—both before, during and after any affair you may choose to have. That you don't rub my face in it.'

'This is extraordinary,' he breathed, raking his fingers back through his shorn hair which, thankfully, was beginning to grow a little. 'You're basically giving me carte blanche to be unfaithful?'

She didn't appear to be listening, for her gaze was locked to the movement of his hand and he found himself remembering the way she had pressed her fingers into his scalp when she'd been coming, crying out something softly in her own language. He wondered if she had been remembering it too. Hell. Why think about that *now*? He shifted uncomfortably in his chair, thankful that the sudden jerk of his erection was concealed by the snowy fall of the tablecloth. But his thoughts quickly shifted from desire to evaluation. He tried to imagine how other men in his position would react if confronted with the astounding fact that their wife-to-be was prepared to look the other way, if he were ever unfaithful. But her words gave him no heady rush of freedom or anticipation—in fact, his overriding feeling was one of indignation and a slowly simmering anger.

'Why, Zabrina?' he demanded. 'Are you planning to do the same? To take other men as your lovers and expect me to be understanding in turn?'

'Of course not! If you want the truth, I can't imagine ever wanting any other man but you.'

He sat back in his chair, surprised by her candour. This wasn't the first time this particular sentiment had been expressed to him by a woman—yet instead of his usual irritation he found himself ridiculously pleased by her sweet honesty. 'I see,' he said, again.

'Obviously I would prefer our marriage to be monogamous, because I've seen the havoc these affairs can wreak. I've seen the damage they can inflict on a couple's relationship.' She tore off a fragment of croissant and lifted it to her mouth before seeming to change her mind and putting it back down on the plate again. Her eyes were very dark and very direct. 'And since we're on the subject. You haven't told me anything about your own parents.'

Instantly he was on the defensive. 'There's nothing much to tell. It's all on the record, as I'm sure you know. I imagine you've seen it for yourself.' Roman could feel his throat thicken and cursed the pain one woman's desertion could still cause him. No wonder he never talked about it. No wonder he had closed his mind to it a long time ago. 'My mother left when I was three years old and I never saw her again,' he said baldly. 'My father never remarried.'

'But—'

'But what?' he interrupted, forcing all the bitter emotion from his words and replacing it with a tone of cool finality. He reminded himself that this was a conversation they needed to have only once and he could make it as short as he wanted. 'Those are the facts, Zabrina. I've never gone in for analysis and I don't intend to start now.' He stared down at the inky brew in his coffee cup before lifting his gaze to hers. 'And since we're being so remarkably frank, there's something else we should address. I think we both need to know where we stand on the subject of divorce, don't you?'

Zabrina grew still as his words filtered across the table towards her, stabbing at her like little arrows. She should have been prepared for this question but, stupidly, she wasn't and as a result she found herself filled with another rush of uncertainty. Had she thought that if she was so reasonable on the subject of fidelity, Roman might declare she would be his wife for life? And wasn't there some inexplicable part of her which *wanted* that—because while she might feel unsettled around him, weirdly she felt really *safe*? As if Roman could protect her from some of the terrors of the world. That as long as he was by her side, nothing really bad could happen.

Why think something as irrational as that?

She stared at the sunny gleam of her half-eaten mango, trying to work out what had changed inside her, but it was difficult to put her finger on, mainly because she didn't understand the softening of her feelings towards the man she was soon to marry. It wasn't just the amazing sex they'd shared on the train—although that had obviously been the most incredible thing which had ever happened to her. It was more to do with his subsequent behaviour and the conversations they shared whenever they took their meals together. He spoke to her as if she were his equal. She realised that sometimes Roman could seem as sympathetic as 'Constantin' had been. He made her feel as if her views counted. As if she was an intelligent person worthy of consideration. And nobody had ever done that before.

But that didn't mean she should allow herself to be lulled into a false sense of security, because, although his attitude towards her might sometimes be sympathetic, his feelings hadn't changed. He didn't *have* feelings towards her, remember? Of *course* he would wish to address the subject of divorce, because it was relevant. This wasn't an emotional discussion, she reminded herself, but a practical one. They were a modern monarchy and there wasn't a royal family in the world which hadn't been affected by marital breakdown. Divorce no longer held any real stigma—other than the devastating heartbreak her auntie had told her about after she'd gone through it herself. Perhaps that was what had made her mother so determined to hang onto her own marriage, no matter what. And surely she couldn't be condemned for that.

'I don't know about you,' she said, meeting the question in his eyes, 'but I would prefer to avoid divorce, especially if there are children involved. Though obviously,' she amended hurriedly, 'if circumstances were to change—'

'In what sense?' he questioned coolly.

The words were threatening to stick in the back of her throat, so that each one felt as if it had been coated with tar. 'If, say, you were to meet another woman,' she began. 'And to fall in love with her. Then obviously I wouldn't stand in your way, if you wanted to end the marriage.'

His face was shuttered. 'How very understanding of you, Zabrina. I had no idea I was marrying such a libertarian.'

'Why, what would you prefer me to do?' she demanded. 'Display an undignified rage and rake your cheeks with my fingernails?'

'Honestly?' He gave a short laugh. 'Right now what I would prefer you to do involves being locked in my arms.'

But it was less of a question and more of a statement and the short silence which followed was broken by the smooth glide of his chair against the marble floor. Zabrina's heart began to thunder and she felt the curl of excitement low in her belly as he rose to his feet.

'Roman,' she said—and this too was a statement, because he was walking around the table towards her, moving with a natural grace and stealth which was incredible to watch, and the look of intent on his sensual features cried out to something deep inside her. Something which scared and excited her. She tried to bat the feelings away but somehow it wasn't working. Beneath her silk dress, she could feel her nipples tightening into hard buds and surely he must be able to see that too? There was a syrupy tug in her belly and suddenly she longed for him to touch her there. She swallowed and felt her cheeks colour.

Yes, *there*—where the aching was at its most intense. Did he see her blush? Was that why his lips curved into that seeking smile?

He was beside her now. Reaching down and lifting her clean off the chair—or was she reaching up to him? She didn't know, and afterwards she would find it impossible to remember. All she knew was that there were no servants present—for he had dismissed them all—and that this was the first time they had been alone since she had stepped off that train in Rosumunte.

And that they seemed to be in the middle of some crazy sexual power game.

'Roman,' she whispered.

'We're done talking,' he husked. 'Just kiss me.'

It was an uneven request which went straight to her heart but Zabrina needed no such instruction because her lips were already seeking his, and, oh, that first touch of his skin against hers made her gasp. How could a simple kiss feel like this? How come that already she wanted to explode with pleasure? One of his hands was tangled in the fall of her hair while the other was on her peaking breast, his thumb circling the pebbled nipple with dextrous provocation which was making her want to squirm. Sanity implored her to call a halt but she couldn't. She didn't want to.

Her hands explored the width of his powerful shoulders then reacquainted themselves with his chest, her nails scraping hungrily against the fine linen of his shirt. She could feel the faint whorl of hair against his muscular torso and, as he cupped his palms possessively over her buttocks, he deepened the kiss. He was pulling her even closer, so that his body was imprinted on hers. She felt the rocky outline of his erection and remembered what it had been like when he had been naked and proud, and she shuddered in his arms.

'Sweet heaven,' he husked, and never had she thought that a man so powerful could sound so helpless. 'How the hell do you do that?'

'Do what?'

'I don't know,' he grated, almost angrily, as he circled his hips against her, his voice dipping to a silken murmur. 'Do you like that?'

'You know I do,' she whispered back.

The words seemed to stir him into action, for he began to move. He was backing her across the room, his mouth not leaving hers, until she could feel the coolness of the wall pressing against her back. His mouth was on her neck. Her jaw. As she looped her arms around his neck and arched herself into the hardness of his body he gave a low laugh, and the sound of his exultation thrilled her even more. And now his fingers were rucking up her dress and lightly tracking over the goose-pimples which were rippling over her thighs. Any minute now and he would reach her panties, whose moist panel felt like an unbearable barrier, denying him the access she was so desperate to grant him. She squirmed in expectation and he gave an unsteady laugh.

'Do you have any idea of how much I want you, Princess?' he bit out in a tone she'd never heard him use before, and in that moment Zabrina felt a wave of the same heady power which had flooded her the first time he'd made love to her. *She* could make him feel like this.

But that random thought was her undoing—or maybe her salvation.

Because he hadn't 'made love' to her, had he?

He'd had sex with her while pretending to be someone else! He'd thought—and presumably still did—that she had a comprehensive backlist of lovers! He'd tried to wriggle out of marrying her!

Reality shattered the tension like a rock hurled through a window, but she tried to block it because she didn't want to think about those things right now. She didn't want to destroy the pleasure she was feeling. But, infuriatingly, she couldn't keep them at bay any longer—and one thought dominated everything. Wasn't this just another example of Constantin/Roman amusing himself with her as if she were his own, personal plaything? And was she prepared to go along with that?

No, she was not.

Somehow Zabrina untangled herself from his arms and took a step sideways, needing to put some space between them, terrified that any closer and she'd be tempted to carry on. But hot on her frustration came a sudden wave of irritation when she saw just how *composed* Roman looked. Why, he might have been doing nothing more strenuous than reading the financial pages of the newspaper!

'That's enough,' she said, in a low voice.

'So I see. But you're not going to deny how much you were enjoying that, are you?' he challenged softly.

Oh, if only that were the case—but Zabrina was no hypocrite. She wished she knew what she wanted. Or what she didn't want. Deep down she wanted to make a success of this arranged marriage, but everything seemed to be in such a muddle. *She* was in a muddle and she didn't know what do.

She wanted to burst into tears and laugh out loud, all at the same time. She wanted to rush from the breakfast room—yet she wanted him to lock the door and finish what they had started. But she mustn't. She really mustn't. The King of Petrogoria had spent the last week treating her with polite and considered detachment. He hadn't shown a single jot of desire for her. He had behaved as if she were some convalescing relative who'd come to stay at the palace, not the flesh and blood woman he was soon to marry. Only now he seemed to have become bored with that particular course of action—and presumably that was why he had kissed her. Was this all some sort of game to him? Did he think she was like one of those old-fashioned dolls her grandmother used to have—the ones you wound up so they would obediently walk and talk for you?

'You know I was enjoying it. But we both know the rules. Or rather, I thought we did. No…' Her voice trembled a little but she forced herself to say it. Why be shy of saying something they'd actually *done*? 'No sex until we're officially man and wife.'

'That didn't seem to bother you on the train, Zabrina.'

'I wasn't… I wasn't thinking straight on the train,' she said, smoothing the crumpled skirt of her dress with palms which were clammy. 'And we were lucky not to have been caught. We might not be so lucky this time. So if you'll excuse me, I'm going. I want to get down to the stables before my dress fitting and check everything is ready for Midas's arrival.'

'As you wish.' He was looking at her thoughtfully—as if he knew perfectly well that her composure was nothing but a façade. But the hard gleam of his eyes was underpinned with something else and she couldn't quite work out what it was. 'Oh, and I'm going away for a few days.'

And Zabrina was surprised by the sudden sinking of her heart. He was going away without her, leaving her alone in the palace? 'Where?'

'I'm taking a short trip to the Marengo Forest. I want to meet with a few people there so we can get the ball rolling on the airport development as soon as the wedding takes place.'

She nodded her head. Of *course* his mind was

fixed on his shiny new acquisition—wasn't that the main reason he would soon be sliding a golden band on her finger? And, while he might have been momentarily distracted by that passionate encounter, he wasn't obsessing about it, like her. He wasn't reading all kinds of things into it which simply didn't exist. So show him how independent you can be. Don't be such a *limpet*. She nodded. 'In that case, I'll see you when you get back. Have a good trip.'

He had started walking ahead and when Zabrina realised he was pulling rank on her, she had to resist a childish urge to race him to the door! But just as he reached the door, he briefly turned his dark head.

'Oh, by the way, you'll find some jewellery waiting when you get back to your suite.'

'What kind of jewellery?'

'Just a necklace. I thought you could wear it to the palace ball on Saturday.'

CHAPTER TEN

'*JUST*' A NECKLACE, Roman had said. But this wasn't just any old necklace, Zabrina had quickly realised. This was a glitzy waterfall of sparkling emeralds and diamonds which was too big and too heavy and completely swamped her. But she supposed it was exactly the sort of accessory people would expect a future queen to wear and she had to admit that the jewels matched perfectly her green ball gown. And how strange it was that as she had slithered into the silk creation earlier, she had felt a slow building of anticipation rather than dread. From someone who had hated dresses she had found herself wondering if Roman would approve of her outfit. It came as something of a shock to realise she was dressing for *him*.

The candlelit ballroom was decked with fragrant white roses and now, as the remains of the seven-course banquet were cleared away and the Petrogorian Chamber Orchestra started to play, Roman led her from the table to begin the dancing. The other guests had formed a circle around the dance floor like spectators at a bullfight, to watch the newly engaged couple on their first formal outing. But Zabrina was aware that every eye in the golden ballroom was fixed on *her*. People's gazes were running over her assessingly. Possibly critically. She worried that the high-flown members of Petrogorian society wouldn't approve of the Princess who was shortly to become their Queen. She found herself wishing she'd worn higher shoes because she barely reached Roman's shoulder and surely the discrepancy in their height must make them look faintly bizarre as a couple.

Her sudden attack of anxiety wasn't helped by the recognition that some of the most beautiful women she'd ever seen were gathered in this sumptuous ballroom, along with their powerful husbands. But her smile hadn't faltered as line after line of Roman's loyal subjects had filed in front of her before dinner, and the Prime Minister had seemed favourably impressed when she'd quoted from one of his country's ancient poets.

Zabrina could feel the loud skitter of her pulse as Roman put his arms around her and she tried not to let her inner excitement show too much. The King had been away in the Marengo Forest for three whole days and she was taken aback by how pleased she'd been to see him again. To touch him again. Wasn't it crazy how being on a dance floor allowed you to be intimate with a man in a way which would be forbidden anywhere else? And she had missed him. Missed him more than she should have done, considering she'd barely known him a fortnight. More than anything, she wanted to talk to him because they'd been seated at opposite sides of the table during the sumptuous banquet and had barely exchanged a word all evening.

'So, when did you get back?' she asked a little breathlessly as they began to move in time to the music, because she was acutely aware of the indentation of his fingers at her waist.

'This morning.'

'Oh.' A stupid sense of disappointment washed over her. He'd been here all day and hadn't bothered to let her know? She wanted to say, *Why didn't you come and find me?* Or, *Why didn't you join me for lunch?* But maybe that would have been presumptuous. As if she were laying down terms, or revealing expectations he might stubbornly refuse to meet if he were aware of them. Instead she strove to find just the right, light touch. To sound like the kind of undemanding partner he might wish to spend more time with and not one who was immediately haranguing him with demands. 'I've been with Midas for most of the day.'

'I know you have.' There was a pause. 'I came down to the stables to see you.'

She turned her face upwards, aware of the faintly shadowed jut of his jaw and the sensual curve of his lips. 'But you didn't come over and say hello?'

'You looked as if you were preoccupied. I didn't want to disturb you. I watched you riding for a while and that kept me…entertained. You are quite something on the back of a horse, Zabrina.'

Something in his tone spooked her—but not nearly as much as the thought of Roman quietly observing her, his pewter eyes glinting from within the concealment of the stable yard's many shadows. She wondered how long he had been there for. She wondered if she would have behaved any differently if she'd known he was watching.

'How was the Marengo?' she said, changing the subject.

'The Marengo was fine,' he replied evenly. And then, 'You didn't tell me that your groom was planning on coming to Petrogoria, too.'

She stiffened a little. 'That's because I didn't know.'

'You didn't *know*?'

'Well, that's not strictly true. Not specifically. I knew one of the grooms would travel with him and Stefan has known Midas since he was a foal, so I guess it made sense that he should have been the one to make the journey. But when he got here…well.' She shrugged, feeling the heavy weight of the jewels scratching against her skin and she wished she could just rip them from her neck and drop them to the ground. 'It seemed silly for him to go back immediately, so I gave him permission to stay. Just to get the horse properly settled in, of course.'

'Of course,' echoed Roman, his words noncommittal as he spun her round, thinking that she was as light as a cloud. He glanced down at the loose dark hair which spilled over her shoulders. At the dark green silk which clung to her slender frame, making her appear pristine and perfectly princess-like, especially when adorned by the priceless glitter of his gift. He contrasted that with the carefree image he had seen on horseback earlier, trotting out of the yard with a banner of a ponytail floating behind her. She had tipped back her head and laughed at something her groom had said and something dark and nebulous had invaded his soul. Something which had been eating him up ever since.

Was it jealousy?

No. He felt the slippery silk of her dress beneath his fingertips and his jaw tightened. It couldn't be.

But just because you'd never felt something before, didn't mean you wouldn't be able to recognise it when you did. And if that *were* the case didn't he only have himself to blame? Despite not being the sort of princess he had ever imagined himself marrying, she had persuaded him into going ahead with the union and he had allowed himself to be persuaded, because the pros had outweighed the cons. Or so he had convinced himself. Theirs was to be an unemotional business arrangement. He knew that and she knew that. She had implied that she was prepared to be 'reasonable' if he sought solace in the arms of another woman, as kings had done from the beginning of time, and by implication that meant he couldn't rule out her doing the same, despite her protestations to the contrary. So why did he feel the primitive throb of dark possession when he even considered that option? Why did he want to roar out his anguish at the thought of her ever being in another man's arms?

But his face betrayed nothing, for an implacable countenance had been drummed into him for as long as he could remember. A king must never show his feelings and, in order to guarantee that, it was preferable not to have those feelings in the first place. It had been one of the first things his father had taught him when he had woken on that bleak, black morning to find his mother gone.

It had been a useful lesson in survival.

'Do you want me to ask him to leave?' Zabrina was saying. 'Is that what you want?'

He looked down, steeling himself against the forest-dark beauty of her eyes and resenting the fact that he found her so enchanting, even while inside he was quietly simmering with rage. 'This isn't supposed to be about what *I* want, Zabrina,' he said coolly. 'This is supposed to be your home, not a prison, and if you want your groom to stay on then that, of course, is your prerogative.'

The music came to an end and the Petrogorian Prime Minister stepped in to ask Zabrina to dance and willingly she resumed her progress around the floor with the portly leader, even though she wanted to stay with Roman and ask him…

She swallowed.

Ask him what? He was being perfectly reasonable, wasn't he? Telling her she was free to do as she
wished. Telling her Stefan could stay as long as she
wanted. She didn't imagine it would go down very
well if she started quizzing him about why he was
adopting that tone of voice.

What tone of voice was that?

Dark?

Disapproving?

Yes, both those things.

But if he felt that way, then surely that was his
problem. If she tried to accommodate him—to gauge
his mood and to modify her behaviour accordingly—
wouldn't that be setting an awful precedent, turning
her into the kind of woman she didn't really like? Or
respect. And it wasn't going to be that kind of marriage, she told herself firmly. A meeting of minds and
bodies, hopefully, yes, but ultimately it was a trans-
action. She needed to keep her independence and
sense of self-worth, or else she suspected she could
easily fall into a deep hole of useless yearning for
someone who saw her simply as a means to an end.

She did her best to put on a credible show as a
future queen that night—her mother would have
been proud of her. She danced with everyone who
asked but made sure she conversed with plenty of
the women too, admiring their gowns and jewels
and talking about various charitable endeavours. But
with Roman there was no more dancing. She told
herself it wasn't deliberate and that she was imagin-

ing his cool and sudden distancing himself from her. But as the clock chimed out midnight, and she and the King left the ballroom to the tumultuous applause of their guests, Zabrina realised that she hadn't really had a chance to talk to him again.

Servants converged on them, walking both ahead and behind as they made their stately progress towards her suite. But when they arrived outside her door, Zabrina turned to the King, licking her lips and slanting him a nervous smile. 'I wonder, shall we have a…nightcap?'

If she had suggested that he suddenly broke into an impromptu rendition of the Petrogorian national anthem, he couldn't have looked more—not *shocked*, exactly, but certainly slightly appalled. As if she had just come out with a highly irregular proposition and had somehow let herself down.

'Unfortunately that will not be possible. I have work which I need to attend to,' he said coolly, briefly lifting her fingers to his lips and bowing his dark head as he kissed them. 'I will see you at breakfast tomorrow.'

The imprint of his mouth on her hand was all too brief and suddenly Silviana was ushering her inside and helping remove her necklace, before undoing all the little buttons at the back of her ball gown.

'Shall I run you a bath before you retire, mistress?' she ventured.

Zabrina shook her head. 'No, thank you. To be honest, I'd just like to be left on my own now.'

'Is something…forgive me for my presumption, Your Royal Highness, but is something *wrong*?'

Zabrina was biting the inside of her lip but she forced herself to smile. Because what if she answered that question honestly? What if she dared to admit even to herself that she was scared of the way Roman could make her feel? She didn't want his disapproval and yet she didn't want to go seeking his approval like some tame puppet. So where did that leave her?

'No, nothing is wrong.' She widened her smile, hoping it looked more reassuring than it felt. 'It's just been a long day and that was my first official introduction as Roman's future bride.'

'All the servants were saying how fine you looked, mistress,' cooed Silviana. 'And that you will make a wonderful queen.'

'That's very sweet of them. Go now and make sure you get a good rest. You've waited up very late.'

But once the servant had left, Zabrina found herself unable to relax and, even though she undressed and climbed into bed, the adrenalin which was rushing around her body made it impossible for her to sleep. She stared at the ceiling. She stared at the necklace which lay discarded on her dressing table, the pile of stones glittering in the moonlight like a handful of shattered glass.

She thought about Roman, working in his office, no doubt. And then she thought about Midas— because that was easier on her heart than thinking about Roman—and was suddenly overcome with an urgent need to see her beloved horse. She could put her arms around his neck and give him the kind of unconditional love she'd never felt comfortable channelling anywhere else apart from to her siblings.

Sliding on a pair of jodhpurs and a fine wool sweater, she slipped silently from her room, listening for a moment as the door opened soundlessly, her gaze darting down the wide marble corridor. But there was nobody around and maybe that wasn't so odd. Servants had to sleep.

She made her way towards the stables, moving as noiselessly as she could and sticking mainly to the shadows but thankfully encountering nobody along the way. Outside in the fresh air the moon was still waxing—every night getting bigger and brighter—and the stable yard was bathed in ghostly silver. Ignoring the heavy sounds of breathing and occasional snorts coming from the King's thoroughbred horses, Zabrina made her way to Midas's loose box and peered inside.

To her surprise, the horse was lying down, fast asleep—which meant that he must be much more contented in his new home than she'd imagined. But he must have had one ear pricked up and heard her, for he instantly picked himself up and came over to nuzzle her. She petted him for long minutes, murmuring to him in Albastasian sweet talk, and felt much better as a result. It was only when she decided that she really did need to get some sleep and reluctantly began to walk back towards the palace that she saw a silhouette standing motionless on the other side of the yard. She did not jump but carried on walking towards the shadowed figure because she assumed…and that was her first mistake.

'Stefan?' she whispered. 'Is that you?'

'Why, is that who you were hoping for?'

Instantly, Zabrina knew who was speaking and it wasn't Stefan. Because although the groom was young and articulate, he did not speak with a velvety Petrogorian accent, nor have such an aristocratic delivery. Nor would his words ever have been tinged with unmistakable accusation.

'Roman,' she breathed.

He stepped out of the shadows and she was appalled by her body's instant response to all that powerful masculinity, because surely her overwhelming emotion in such a scenario shouldn't be one of desire… He was still wearing the formal suit he'd had on at the ball, though she noticed he had removed his tie and loosened the collar. Just as she noticed the brooding quality of his darkened features and the censure which hardened his sensual lips.

'Surprised?' he taunted softly.

'A little. Have you been spying on me, Roman?'

'You dare to accuse *me*?'

'Too right I do! I want to know what you're doing here. Why you suddenly sprang out of nowhere at this hour.'

'But you weren't scared, were you? You didn't

scream and raise the alarm as many women in your situation would have done.'

'So I am to be rebuked for reacting maturely and not like some hysteric?'

'Don't try and change the subject!'

'Then perhaps you could try getting to the point. How did you know where I'd be?'

'Did you really think you could wander the palace at the depths of night without being detected by anyone, Zabrina? That my corridors would go unguarded and my servants not have your welfare at heart?' He gave a bitter laugh as his gaze flicked over her. 'When one of Andrei's aides came rushing to my office and told me that the Princess was out exploring at the dead of night, I knew immediately where you'd be.'

Her heart was thumping painfully but she tried to put a flippant face on it. 'Really? Since you're not a practising clairvoyant as far as I'm aware, perhaps you'd like to let me into the secret of how you "knew" where to find me.'

'Where is he, Zabrina?'

She wanted to say *Who?* but she knew exactly who he meant and to pretend she didn't would surely imply guilt. 'I suppose you're talking about Stefan,' she said slowly. 'What did you imagine, Roman— that I would creep down here to have sex with my groom at the first available opportunity?'

He flinched. 'Did you?' he grated and Zabrina

wondered if she had imagined the shudder of pain in his voice.

She stared at him, not bothering to hide her incredulity. Did he really think she'd be interested in a man like Stefan—indeed, in any man—when the only one she had ever wanted was standing right across the yard from her? What kind of women had he dealt with in the past if his level of distrust was so deep and so instant?

'I am hugely insulted,' she said, her voice shaking, 'that you have made so many negative assumptions about me and should believe me capable of such terrible behaviour. What makes you think so badly of me, Roman?'

There was a long pause before he answered, his voice seeming to draw each word out reluctantly. 'I told you. Rumours about you had started reaching me a few months ago—rumours which ignited my curiosity.'

'You mean that I was occasionally guilty of voicing my own opinion?'

'Yes, that.' He narrowed his eyes. 'But I find that trait is not as unappealing as I imagined it would be.'

'Wow,' she said sarcastically. 'This is progress indeed. But much as I would like to applaud your sudden emergence from the Dark Ages, I'm more interested to know what else it was you heard about me.'

He shrugged. 'That you had a habit of disappearing. That the Princess Zabrina would sometimes ride out at first dawn with her groom and not return until the noon sun was high in the sky.'

'And so you came to the conclusion that Stefan and I were galloping off together to enjoy some sort of illicit encounter?'

'Something like that.'

'How dare you? How dare you accuse me of such a thing, Roman?' All pretence at light-heartedness now abandoned, her voice had begun shaking with rage. 'Do you really think I could be so duplicitous that I would agree to marry one man, while being intimate with another?'

'Of course I can!' he flared. 'Because you had sex with Constantin, didn't you, Zabrina? You weren't thinking about Roman then, were you? So how can you explain that?'

She spoke without thinking. She spoke from the heart. 'I can't,' she said simply.

There was a pause. 'Neither can I.'

They stared at each other in silence and all Zabrina could see was the gleam of the moon in his shadowed eyes.

'I tried to resist you,' she said quietly. 'Or rather, I tried to resist Constantin, because I had never met anyone like him before. Surely you must have noticed how deliberately rude and abrupt I was towards you at the beginning?'

'I thought that was a game you were playing.' He gave a short laugh. 'Don't you realise that a headstrong and stubborn woman is exceedingly attractive to a man?'

She shook her head. 'I don't know what happened to me that night and I don't really want to think about it now. But I hold my hands up—I *did* used to ride out with Stefan. If you really want to know what I was doing, then I'll tell you—but we certainly weren't having sex.'

'Really?' He spoke carelessly, but Roman could do nothing about the sudden punch of hope to his heart, even though he despised his visceral reaction to her words.

She nodded and in the moonlight he saw her face assume an expression of fierceness. 'In my country I had a list of charities of which I was patron and which my sister Daria is going to take over, now that I'm no longer there. I was obviously invested in all those charities but there was one in particular which was very close to my heart. It was…' She hesitated. 'It was a refuge on the outskirts of the city. A refuge for women who have suffered domestic violence.'

His eyes narrowed. 'So why all the cloak-and-dagger stuff?'

She nodded, as if this was a topic with which she was familiar. As if she was used to accusation.

'My parents didn't approve of my involvement with these women. It was something else they turned a blind eye to. To admit that women suffered at the hands of men and were made impoverished if ever they chose to escape from abusive relationships—

well, they were both of the opinion that the women didn't try hard enough to save their marriages!'

'Good heavens,' said Roman faintly.

The look she threw him was challenging. 'What, is that a bit hardcore old-fashioned, even for you?'

He didn't like being held up as someone completely out of touch with the modern world, just as he didn't like the way she was looking at him. It made him feel...*uncomfortable.* Kings were rarely forced to say they were sorry but Roman knew he needed to say it now. 'I shouldn't have leapt to those conclusions,' he said gruffly. 'Will you forgive me?'

Her absolution wasn't instant. She waited just long enough for him to entertain a little doubt in his mind—and didn't part of him admire her for her strength of character?

Eventually, she nodded. 'Yes, I forgive you,' she said. 'But, going forward, I'd prefer it if you didn't just leap to conclusions. And that it's probably better if you don't just brood about something, but ask me outright.'

She smiled then and the deepening dimple in her cheek drew his gaze, so that suddenly it looked like the most beautiful thing he had ever seen.

Roman swallowed. Her lips were gleaming irresistibly and looking unbearably kissable. He knew what he should do. Escort her back to her suite and bid her goodnight. Just as he knew what he wanted to do, which was to pull her into his arms and then lay her down in one of the dark corners of the stables and make love to her over and over again. And then he thought of all the reasons why he shouldn't—but the one which dominated them all was duty.

Duty.

It was a word which had been drummed into him from the moment he'd been born. A concept which had driven him all his life. It had been duty which had made him focus himself on his lessons and fencing skills, rather than give in to the bitter tears of a deserted child. Duty which had made him fulfil his end of this marriage bargain with the young Albastasian Princess.

Couldn't he—for once—take a break from the crushing weight of royal expectations? Suddenly, he felt a jolt of his own power as he looked at her. 'I want so badly to make love to you.'

He saw her bite her lip and gaze at the ground, as if seeking an answer amid the strands of silvered straw which lay there, and when she raised her head again, her face was serene and very solemn, as if she had come to some swift conclusion of her own. 'I want that, too.'

He sucked in an unsteady breath, his body warming as he acknowledged her instant capitulation. 'And I suspect that if I drew you into the shadows now and laid my hands and my lips upon your body,' he continued, 'you would again be mine.'

'R-Roman,' she said shakily, but she didn't contradict him.

'But we aren't going to do that.'

'We…aren't?'

Was he wrong to enjoy her obvious disappointment? No, he was not. For didn't her response indicate that the balance of power between them was more equal than he'd thought, and perhaps that was something he needed to address.

'No, we aren't.' He paused just long enough to give *her* a taste of doubt, because wasn't uncertainty one of the most powerful aphrodisiacs of all? 'Instead, I will come to your suite tomorrow. At midnight.'

Her eyes widened. 'But you can't! You know you can't. Tradition states—'

'I don't give a damn what tradition states because *I* am King now and I make the rules.' He lowered his voice, even though there was nobody within earshot. 'I have no intention of broadcasting my movements to palace staff but neither do I intend to have sex with you on a sofa, or rammed up against a wall, or lying on the dusty ground of the stables, even though the prospect of not doing that right now is almost unendurable. I want to share your bed—properly. As Roman, not Constantin. As the man I am and not the man I was pretending to be. But I need you to be certain that this is what you want too, Zabrina.' He paused. 'This is to be no hot-blooded and hasty liaison, fuelled by rampant hormones and frustration, which is why I'm giving you adequate time to think about it. Because if, for any reason, you decide that you would prefer to wait for our wedding night to be intimate with me again then you must send me a signal.'

'How?'

His eyes gleamed like the blade of a sword. 'If you wish me to share your bed, then you should light a lamp in your window tomorrow night, and leave it unshuttered. If the light flares, then I will come to you. But if shutters are closed then I will not, and we will never refer to the matter again. It will be as though we never had this conversation. Do you understand what I'm saying to you, Zabrina?'

'Yes,' she said, in a voice so quiet he could barely hear her response. 'I understand.'

CHAPTER ELEVEN

ZABRINA SHIVERED AS she positioned the light in the centre of her bedroom window, thinking how strange life was. One minute you could be watching a film about a mermaid and wondering how she could possibly keep her hair looking that shiny when it was constantly immersed in salt-water, and the next...

She licked her dry lips.

Next you could be sending out a secret and silent message as you waited for your lover.

And she didn't have a clue what she was getting herself into.

Should she be in bed, waiting for Roman to arrive? Surely it wouldn't be a very attractive sight if she were caught anxiously pacing the floor—even if she *was* clad in a delicate nightgown which she had plucked from her trousseau with trembling fingers. Maybe she ought to be in bed, carefully positioned against the pillows, with her newly washed hair falling artfully over her shoulders. No. No, she couldn't do that. She would feel like a fraud—an imposter—

and it would make the situation even more unreal than it already was.

There was a light rap on the door and then, without any prompting from her, it silently opened and closed again and there was Roman in her suite, dominating the space around him, dominating everything with his aura of alpha masculinity. For a moment Zabrina said nothing—but her breathing was so erratic she doubted she'd be able to speak any kind of sense in any case. Because, as always, his brooding beauty stopped her in her tracks. For once his muscular body was clothed in muted colours—presumably so he would melt into the background as he made his way from his part of the palace to hers. But no matter what he wore, his aristocratic bearing always shone through, like a diamond in a pile of rubble.

Yet her own royal status suddenly seemed to count for nothing. She felt like a fraud despite standing before him in her provocative lingerie, which was presumably perfect for an assignation such as this. But how she looked on the outside wasn't how she felt on the inside. Her fluttery excitement kept morphing into worry that she wouldn't be able to handle the way he made her feel, because wasn't the underlying message she was getting from him that this was supposed to be about sex, not emotion?

The King probably thought she knew how these midnight encounters worked, when the truth was she didn't have a clue. So did she have to go through another humiliating disclosure about her lack of experience and hope he'd believe her this time—or did she pretend, and try to pick things up as they went along?

Yet wasn't the whole point of their relationship supposed to be honesty?

'Roman—'

'Shh. Just let me take you to bed, Princess. Because I don't think I can wait for a moment longer.'

His soft words shushed her. They bathed her in silk. The slight cracking of his voice was hugely flattering and suddenly Zabrina was in his arms and his fingers were pushing back through the spill of her hair and he was kissing her as she'd never been kissed before. Stars splintered at the backs of her eyes as she kissed him back, as if they couldn't get enough of each other. He groaned against her mouth and then suddenly he scooped her up into his arms and carried her into the bedroom, the mattress dipping beneath her as he laid her down on the huge divan.

Without taking his eyes from her face he began to unbutton his shirt, but still she said nothing. For hadn't his soft words been a tacit order not to break the spell of what was about to happen—and wasn't the truth that it really *did* feel like magic?

Zabrina watched as he peeled off his clothes until his golden flesh was naked and rippling in the lamplight. Her mouth dried as he joined her on the bed and he pulled her against his powerful frame. He let out a long sigh as his fingers began to reacquaint themselves with her aching body but there seemed a different kind of urgency about him tonight as he kissed her. Her nerves were quickly dissolved by the sweetness of his mouth roving over her neck, her hair and her breasts and Zabrina was writhing with impatience when at last his hand moved beneath the delicate nightgown and began to ruck up the slippery fabric.

'Was this for your honeymoon night?' he murmured.

'Y-yes,' she whispered back, her skin prickling into goose-bumps.

Did she imagine the brief darkening of his face before he peeled it off with such infinite care, so that in that moment she felt almost...*treasured*? *Cherished*. Zabrina's heart clenched with something which felt unbearably poignant—as if she'd been given a glimpse of something which could never be hers. Something elusive and fragile and wonderful. Was this what *love* felt like? she found herself wondering wistfully. Until she reminded herself fiercely that love was irrelevant. Emotion was superficial and sensation was key to what was happening. So she turned her attention to the satin of his skin, and his deepening kisses indicated just how much she was pleasing him. The pace began to change and quicken. The air crackled with rising tension and musky desire. She felt him reach for protection, heard the rough tearing of foil before he stroked her thighs apart with beguiling fingers. And then he moved over her and she was lost.

Roman groaned as he entered her. She felt so *tight*. Tighter even than she had done on the train—or was that because he was so unbelievably turned on to-night? He thrust deep inside her honeyed flesh, taking her to the brink again and again, until she cried out his name in a ragged plea and he gave her what she wanted. What she needed. What he needed, too. And didn't a distinctly primeval satisfaction wash over him as he heard her shudder out his name, so that he was forced to silence her frantic cries with another kiss? She was still spasming around him when he started coming himself and never had so much seed spilled from his loins before.

Afterwards, drained and empty, he felt the powerful beat of his heart as she lay slumped against his sweat-sheened shoulder, her own hair damp with exertion. He heard the sudden catch in her breathing and wondered if she was crying. And even though it was definitely not his style to probe a woman's mood, he found himself doing it.

'Zabrina?'

She shook her head as if she didn't want to engage. 'Shh,' she said, the sound mimicking the very one he'd made earlier.

It was a get-out clause. An escape route. But surprisingly, Roman paid it no heed. He rolled on top of her again, smoothing the tousled tendrils of hair away from her flushed cheeks. Her eyes were closed as if she didn't want to have this conversation, which would normally have suited him fine, but he found himself unable to ignore the sudden stab of his conscience.

'Zabrina?'

Her lashes fluttered open and he found himself staring into forest-dark eyes.

'I know,' he said softly and nodded his head resolutely. 'I know I was the first man for you. The only man. And I'm sorry I accused you of all those things.'

She drew back, her eyes wide. 'I don't understand.'

'It's hard for me to understand myself.'

'Well, try.'

He traced his forefinger along the tremble of her lips and resisted the urge to kiss them. 'When I saw you waiting for me tonight, you looked so sweet and so nervous.' He shrugged. 'And so obviously out of your depth. You certainly weren't behaving like an experienced woman of the world. Deep down, I realised that on the train, when you told me—only it was easier to think you weren't. To paint you as someone who was wanton, and free.'

'And why was that, Roman?' she questioned softly.

He shook his head, afraid of what he might say, what he might reveal in an unguarded and totally irrelevant post-orgasmic moment. But he had been the one who had started all this, hadn't he?

'Because it would be easier to keep me at a distance?' she guessed, when still he said nothing.

He furrowed his brow into a frown. He didn't want her to be right, just as he didn't want her to be this perceptive. But he wasn't going to tell a lie. 'Maybe,' he admitted. 'And maybe because it gave me permission to make love to you under the guise of another man. I should never have done that, Zabrina.'

'Maybe you shouldn't,' she said slowly. 'But I wanted you to. I wanted it more than I can ever remember wanting anything.'

It was an unexpected display of candour, but to his surprise it didn't repel him or make him want to run. The look in her eyes seemed to be beguiling him even more than before and Roman tensed. The atmosphere was getting claustrophobic and in danger of suffocating him if he wasn't careful.

He swallowed. So what was he going to do about it?

He reached down to play with one of her nipples and felt himself grow hard as it puckered beneath his touch. He kissed her and guided her hand between his legs, biting back a moan of pleasure as she began to whisper featherlight fingertips up and down his aching shaft.

'I want you to teach me,' she said softly. 'About the things you would like me to do.'

Already, he felt as if he could explode. 'You don't seem to need any advice from me. You're doing just fine,' he growled.

He had been about to show her how to pleasure him but it seemed that his princess was an instinctive expert where his body was concerned and a feeling of anticipation rippled over his body as he reached down and began to finger her in turn.

He closed his eyes.

Because this type of feeling he could cope with, but only this.

Maybe that was the only lesson he needed to teach her.

When Zabrina awoke, he had gone. She turned to look at the imprint of his head on the pillow and felt her heart give a wrench. Of course he had gone. That was the deal. He had crept from her bed under the velvety cloak of darkness, to slip back unnoticed through the palace corridors.

Lying amid the warm and rumpled sheets, watching dawn as it filtered through the unshuttered window, she allowed herself a moment of erotic recall.

It had been…

She swallowed.

It had been divine on every level, bar one. She had been nervous about having sex with the King,

wondering if it would be the same as having sex
with his alter-ego bodyguard. But it had been incredible. Perhaps because so many different lay-
ers of their characters had been peeled away, it had
felt deeper than what had happened before. It had
been intense. Powerful. Almost *transforming*. Every
single time. Once, when he had been deep inside
her pulsing out his seed, she had wanted to weep
from pure joy. She had wanted to trace her fingertips over the shadowed graze of his jaw and thank
him for making her feel this way. But instinct had
warned her against such an over-the-top reaction
and instinct had proved her right. Because just before Roman had returned to his own quarters, rising gloriously and boldly naked from the sheets, she
had thought he seemed more...

She frowned as she tried to think of a word to
describe it. Remote, yes—that was it. Almost as if
the intensity of their physical interaction had made
him want to instinctively push her away. Maybe she
was reading too much into it. After all, what did *she*
know about how men behaved once they had shared
a woman's bed? And hadn't his last words been a
husky promise that he would come to her later that
night? She smiled as she plumped up the pillows and
afterwards fell asleep and when next she awoke, the
sun was up and Silviana was busying herself in the
suite, laying out all her clothes for the day.

Leaving her hair loose, she put on a floaty dress

the colour of apple blossoms, but she definitely felt nervous as she walked into the breakfast room, to find Roman already seated and looking at his phone. She wanted him to say something or do something. To send out some secret acknowledgement of what they had shared during the night by slanting her a complicit look. But when he glanced up from his phone and smiled, his face looked nothing except composed.

'Good morning,' he said. 'Did you sleep well?'

Maybe it was irrational but Zabrina was disappointed at the lack of unspoken communication passing between them. She wondered how he'd react if she blurted out the truth. *No, not really. How could I possibly sleep when you were deep inside my body for most of the night?* But, of course, she didn't. She simply sat down while a servant shook out a napkin and placed it on her lap, and attempted to match her fiancé's cool air of self-possession.

'Very well, thank you,' she answered. 'You?'

'Mmm,' he said, non-committal as he put his phone face-down on the table, as if he were making a great sacrifice. 'So, what are you doing today?'

'I have a dress fitting, and I need to finalise the design for the top layer of the wedding cake.' She lifted up her spoon to scoop up a cinnamon-dusted strawberry and shot him a look. 'Would you like to give your input? Any favourite recipes from your childhood?'

His expression suddenly grew stony and shut-tered. 'I've never been much of a cake-eater, Za-brina. So why don't I leave that side of it to you?'

She wanted to ask what had made his face darken like that, but she didn't do that either. The mood in the room was too fragile for those sorts of ques-tions. *She* was too fragile—like a piece of hon-eycomb which had been placed in the path of an approaching pair of feet. The brief insecurity which had washed over her in bed earlier that morning now grew heightened. In a flash it came to her that she wanted more than erotic intimacy. She wanted other intimacies, too. She wanted them to grow close and to be a real couple—not spend her life tiptoeing around his feelings. She looked at the proud jut of his aristocratic jaw.

So make it happen.

Don't crowd him.

In public at least, give him space.

Zabrina dug her spoon into another strawberry and nibbled at the fruit delicately, even though she would have preferred to have picked it up with her fingers. But she knew how palace life worked. Be-neath the careful scrutiny of the servants she would play the royal game which was expected of her. She would make small talk and discuss generalities about the day ahead and that would have to do for the time being. But there was nothing to stop her from break-ing down Roman's barriers whenever she got the opportunity. Surely that was essential if she wanted to discover more about this complex man she was soon to marry.

And where better than when they were alone in bed?

CHAPTER TWELVE

'YOU NEVER REALLY talk about your past, do you, Roman?'

Roman kept his eyes tightly shut, hoping his forbidding body language would stem the Princess's infuriating line of questioning. Because this wasn't the first time she'd tried to quiz him after one of his delicious midnight visits to her bedroom. Chipping away as she tried to get to know him better, as lovers inevitably did—no matter how many times he discouraged them. He guessed that with Zabrina he had been unusually indulgent—and at least their powerful sexual chemistry meant it had been easy to distract her. He'd been able to deflect her annoying queries with a foray into mutual bliss, but this time he heard the note of stubborn determination in her voice which made him suspect the subject wasn't going away.

It didn't.

'Roman?' Soft fingertips began to stroke distracting little circles on his forearm. 'I know you're not asleep.'

Reluctantly, Roman opened his eyes, his vision instantly captured by the sight of the naked woman lying in bed next to him. He felt the instant thunder of his heart as he drank in her slender curves. If this were anyone else he would simply leave but with Zabrina he couldn't—and not just because he was due to marry her in ten days' time. Because wasn't the truth that he simply couldn't bear the thought of leaving her bed? Not when there were still several hours available to them before daybreak, which he intended to put to the best possible use. Starting with the judicious use of his tongue, which he would trickle down over her belly until her nails were scrabbling against his scalp and she was moaning helplessly and bucking beneath him.

But despite the hungry clamour in his groin, his desire was tinged with the flicker of resentment, because he knew that in many ways he had become unexpectedly addicted to her. Didn't he sometimes despair of the way she effortlessly seemed to weave her spell around him? He gave an impatient sigh. Maybe his attempts at evading her questions were simply delaying the inevitable. Maybe his future wife had the right to ask him things which had been forbidden to other lovers.

'Which particular part of my past particularly interests you, Princess?' he questioned coolly.

Her answer came straight back, as if she'd been rehearsing it.

'Your parents.'

'My parents,' he repeated slowly.

'Everyone has them at some point in their life, Roman. You know all about mine but I know nothing about yours. I mean, I know that your father died four years ago and that your parents got divorced, but I don't know any more than that because you've never said.'

'And don't you think there's a reason for that?'

She wriggled up the bed a little, so that her dark hair shimmered down, rather disappointingly concealing the rosy nipple which had been on display.

'So why don't you tell me what that reason is?' she said.

The look in her eyes was compelling, the expression on her face serene as she calmly returned his gaze. And all at once it felt as if there was no hiding place. No place left to run—and the weirdest thing was that Roman didn't *want* to run. He wanted to confide in her. To tell her things he'd never discussed with another soul. A pulse began to beat at his temple. Why *was* that? Why did he suddenly feel as if he had been carrying around an intolerable burden and this was his chance to put it down for a while?

But it wasn't easy to articulate words he'd spent a lifetime repressing, or to expand on them, and for a while he just listened to the sound of silence, broken only by the distant ticking of a clock.

'My mother left when I was three,' he said at last. 'After that, it was just me and my father.'

'What was she like?'

It was a simple question but something he'd never been asked outright and, stupidly, he wasn't expecting it. Forbidden images of a tall blonde woman with a worried face swam into his mind and Roman realised just how long it had been since he'd thought about her. Since he had *allowed* himself to think about her. 'I don't remember very much about her,' he said. 'Only that she used to read me bedtime stories in a low and drawling voice. She was American. She came from Missouri and she used to wear a necklace with a bluebird on it.'

'What else?'

She looked at him and he wondered if her inquisitiveness was inspired by curiosity or horrified fascination. Because a mother who deserted her child always excited people's interest—particularly women's. A mother who left her child was seen as a monster and the child as unloved and unwanted. His preference would have been to have shut the subject down but suddenly he realised that some day he and Zabrina were going to have to explain the lack of a paternal grandmother to their own children, so maybe she *needed* to know. 'What kind of thing do you want to know?'

'Like, how did they meet?'

He raked back through the things he knew, which were surprisingly sketchy. 'They met when my father was on a world tour. She was working as a waitress and I think he just became obsessed by her and swept her off her feet. He proposed, she accepted and he brought her back here with almost indecent haste.' His voice hardened into flint. 'It's why I became an advocate of arranged marriages, Zabrina. He should never have made her his wife.'

She pushed a strand of hair out of her eyes and blinked at him. 'Because she was a commoner?' she said slowly.

'Almost certainly. She couldn't deal with royal life or all the restrictions which accompany it. Or so my father told me afterwards. She never settled into life here—not even when she had me. I remember that sometimes she seemed too scared to hold me and seemed to leave most of my care to my nurse, Olga.' He flinched as the memories came faster now. A black spill of memories he couldn't seem to hold back. 'Even when she read to me at night, she would slip into my room under cover of darkness. I noticed she started being around less and less and sometimes I would spot her heading towards me in one of the corridors, only she would turn away and pretend she hadn't seen me. Don't look at me that way, Zabrina, because it's true. And then one day, she left. She *left*,' he repeated, angry at the hot twist of pain in his heart. Angry with himself because surely it shouldn't still hurt like this. 'She just walked away and never looked back.'

She didn't respond to that and he heaved a breath

of thanks, thinking she'd taken the hint and would ask him no more. He was just about to pull her into his arms and lose himself in the sweetness of her body when she propped herself up on one elbow and screwed up her nose. 'So what happened after that? I mean, how did you find out she'd gone?'

'Is this really necessary?' he demanded.

'I think it's important,' she clarified quietly. 'And I'd like to hear the rest of the story.'

'I'll tell you how I found out.' His voice grew quiet now. So quiet that he saw her lean forward fractionally to hear him. 'I woke up one morning and couldn't find her and when I asked Olga where she was, she told me I must go and speak to my father. So I went downstairs and discovered my father calmly eating breakfast. He looked up and told me my mother had gone and wouldn't be coming back, but I didn't believe him. I remember I ran from the room and he let me go. I remember searching every inch of the palace until I was forced to accept that the King had spoken the truth and she really *had* gone.'

He tried to focus himself back in the present but the memories were too strong and they overwhelmed him like the heavy atmosphere you got just before a storm. He remembered the dry sobs which had heaved from his lungs as he'd hidden himself away in a shadowed corner. He hadn't dared show his heartbreak or his fear, for hadn't his father drummed into him time after time that princes should never show weakness or emotion? Olga had eventually found

him, but he had turned his face to the wall as she'd
tried to tempt him out with his favourite sweets,
still warm from the palace kitchens. But the usually tempting smell of the coconut had been cloying
and it had been many hours before he had relented
enough to take his nurse's hand and accompany her
back to the nursery.

The silence which followed felt like a reprieve,
but not for long because Zabrina's soft voice washed
over him with yet another question.

'And did you ever hear from your mother again?
I mean, surely she must have written to you. Sent a
forwarding address so you could contact her.'

'Yes, I had an address for her,' he confirmed bitterly. 'And I used to write her letters. At first they
were simple, plaintive notes, asking when she was
coming back.' It made him curl up with disgust to
think how he had humiliated himself by begging her
to return, seeking solace from a woman who had re-
jected him outright. 'After a while, I just used to send
her drawings I'd made, or tell her about my horse, or
my fencing lessons.'

'But you never heard back?'

Was that disapproval he could hear in her voice,
or incredulity? Or just the loathsome pity he had always refused to tolerate? 'No, I never heard back,' he
clipped back and then shrugged. 'So in the end, I just
gave up. My father never remarried, and brought me
up to the best of his ability. It wasn't great. He wasn't
a particularly easy man and it certainly wasn't what

you'd call a normal, nuclear family but we adapted, as people do.'

'And, of course, you had Olga.'

He didn't answer straight away, just stared out of the window, noticing that the silver moon was almost full. 'No. Actually, I didn't.'

It was the first time she had looked truly taken aback. 'But—'

'My father sacked her.'

'He *sacked* her?'

The lump in his throat made it hard for him to speak, yet somehow the words just kept coming. 'He thought we were too close. As he explained, Olga was a servant and she didn't seem to know her place where I was concerned. He said you couldn't have a nursemaid who was acting like a quasi-mother and, anyway, he was done with commoners.'

'Oh, Roman, I'm so sorry,' she breathed, and he steeled himself not to react to the crack of compassion in her voice. 'That's terrible.'

'No, it was not terrible. It was manageable,' he said fiercely, daring her to contradict him, because he didn't want to dwell on the pain of that double rejection or how cold and how empty his life had seemed afterwards. 'After that I had a series of nurses and nannies who looked after me—sometimes men and sometimes women—all of them experts in one field or another.' But despite the variety of staff who had been engaged to help with his upbringing, they all had one thing in common. They never hugged him.

Rarely touched him. Sometimes he'd suspected they'd been instructed to behave that way, but he didn't investigate further because the thought of that made him feel slightly sick. And anyway he didn't care, for in the end it had done him a favour and allowed him to view his brave new world with different eyes. Because at least you knew where you were with those people. *They* would never let you down.

He shot Zabrina a speculative look. 'Satisfied now?' he questioned, not bothering to conceal the note of warning in his voice. 'I don't think there's anything else you need to know.'

Zabrina bit her lip. She was aware he wanted her to leave it—why, his body language couldn't have been more forbidding if he'd tried. But how could she stop asking when there was still so much she didn't know? There were so many gaps in his story and she needed to fill them, because otherwise he would remain a stranger to her and she suspected she might never get another chance like this.

'Is she still alive? Your mother, I mean.'

His body tensed. She thought it looked like rippled marble in the moonlight.

'I have no idea,' he answered coldly. 'I stopped writing when I was thirteen and never heard of her again.'

'And you never tried to have her found, not even when you acceded to the throne? I mean, a king has access to the kind of information which would make that sort of thing easy.'

'Why on earth would I do that, Zabrina?' His lips curved disdainfully. 'Unless you're one of those people who believes that continued exposure to rejection is somehow character forming?'

'And Olga?' she questioned, deciding to ignore his bitter sarcasm. 'What happened to your nurse?'

'That I *did* discover,' he conceded, giving a brief, hard smile. 'She went back to live with her family not far from here, in the mountain town of Posera.'

'And do you—?'

'No! No, that is it!' he interrupted furiously. 'You have tested my patience too long and too far, Zabrina, and I will not be subjected to this any longer!'

Without warning, he rose from the bed and began reaching for the scattered clothes which had been discarded when he had arrived soon after midnight.

'What are you doing?' She was acutely conscious of the note of alarm in her voice but she couldn't seem to keep it at bay.

'What does it look like I'm doing? I'm getting dressed. I'm going back to my own room.'

'But it's still early.'

'I'm perfectly aware what the time is.'

'Roman, there's no need—'

'Oh, but that's where you're wrong, Zabrina. There is every need,' he interjected coldly. 'Because I'm not doing this again. Not ever again.'

'You mean...' She could feel the sudden plummet of her heart. 'You mean you won't be coming to my bed again?'

'I don't know.' There was a pause. 'That's up to you.'

'I don't…' Her fingers dug into the rumpled sheet. 'I don't understand.'

'Don't you?' He waited until he had finished pulling on his soft leather boots before flicking her an emotionless look which had replaced the ravaged expression of before. 'Then let me make it crystal clear for you, just so there won't be any misunderstandings in the future. A future you need to make a decision about, because you need to know which direction you want to take.'

'What are you talking about?' she whispered.

'I'll tell you exactly what I'm talking about. I think we have the makings of a good team,' he said slowly. 'In public we just need to turn up and wave and fulfil the worthwhile causes close to our hearts. And in private I certainly have no complaints about what takes place between us, because I would be the first to admit that you completely blow my mind. But as for the rest.' His face grew dark and brooding again. 'All this other *stuff* you seem intent on dredging up with your endless probing and questioning. That has to stop and it has to stop right now. I'm not interested in analysing the past or its effect on me—because the past has gone. And neither will I contemplate the kind of future where you do nothing but needle away at me. I can't and I won't tolerate such behaviour. Either you accept the man I am today, or the wedding is off. No more questions. No more analysis. Do you understand what I'm saying to you, Zabrina?'

There was a long silence. She could hear the muffled pounding of her pulse as she looked at him. 'That sounds like an ultimatum.'

'Call it what you want. I'm not going to deny it.'

It felt as if someone had taken a heavy, blunt instrument and smashed it into her heart. It was illogical to think he might have reacted any differently, but logic was having no effect on the way his words were making her feel. Zabrina's head was spinning. He had wanted to call off the marriage once before but she had insisted on going through with it because her homeland badly needed this union, and she'd convinced herself they could make the marriage work and produce a family.

But now she could see it wasn't as simple as she'd first thought.

She'd used her parents' marriage as a template for her own behaviour—but she didn't *like* her parents' marriage! Her father's affairs indicated a total lack of respect and regard for his wife and her mother's tacit acceptance of his behaviour was tantamount to a nod of approval. Yet she had calmly told Roman she would be prepared to react in a similar way, because she accepted that was what kings 'did'. Had she been out of her mind? Zabrina's stomach churned. Had she really imagined she'd be content to sit back and watch while Roman behaved that way, when the thought of him having sex with another woman made her want to scream out her horror and her distress?

She realised something else, too. She wanted a real marriage. She wanted to be a wife to Roman in every sense of the word, and for him to be a proper husband. She didn't know if that was possible, but surely she had to give it a try. Because when he had been telling her his sad story about his mother, it had sparked off flickers of recognition inside her. It had made her think of other stories which she had heard so many times before. She might be wrong, but there might be a reason why Roman's mother had disappeared in such a dramatic fashion and maybe she should try to discover if what she suspected was true.

The King was now standing fully dressed in his traditional night-time clothes of jeans and a dark sweater and she could sense the air of impatience radiating from his powerful frame as he waited for her answer. But there was more to Roman than his sometimes intimidating exterior suggested. If she looked beyond his arrogant sense of entitlement, she could detect the deep wound which had been inflicted on him as a boy and which had never been given the chance to heal.

Could she help him do that? Would he accept her help, even if such a thing were possible?

Deliberately she lay back against the pillows. 'I'm not going to address ultimatums—and certainly not when they are delivered in the middle of the night,' she said, with a carelessness she was far from feeling. 'Speak to me about it in the morning.'

She wouldn't have been human if she hadn't enjoyed the very real flash of shock and frustration which gleamed from his eyes—presumably because he was never obstructed quite so openly—before leaving the room without another word. And she suspected he might have slammed the door very loudly, if there hadn't been a continuing need for silence.

CHAPTER THIRTEEN

'SILVIANA?' ZABRINA MADE a final adjustment to the collar of her silk blouse as, with a raised hand, she waylaid her lady-in-waiting just as she was leaving the dressing room. 'Did you ever hear of a palace nurse called Olga?'

The servant lifted her head, her thick, blonde bob swinging around her chin as she did so. Did Zabrina imagine the caution she saw written on her lovely face or was she just getting paranoid?

'Of course I have heard of her, Your Royal Highness. My own mother knew her very well.'

Zabrina nodded. 'I understand she lives in a place called Posera. Is that very far from here?'

Silviana shook her head. 'No, Your Royal Highness. It is a little village nestled in the foothills of the Liliachiun mountains.'

'I was wondering…' Zabrina swallowed, nervous about saying this, but she *needed* to say it. For Roman's sake. For all their sakes. She forced a smile. 'I would like to visit her. This morning. Right now, in fact.'

'Now?' Silviana looked alarmed. 'But you are already late for breakfast with His Imperial Majesty.'

Zabrina shook her head. 'I won't be taking breakfast this morning. Perhaps you could have someone send word to that effect to the King.' And it wasn't just the thought of food which was making her throat close up. She couldn't face walking into the breakfast room under Roman's indifferent gaze and pretend that last night had never happened. Because it had. He had basically told her that if she wasn't prepared to accept the most superficial of marriages, then the wedding was off. *And that was a decision she wasn't prepared to make just yet. Not until she was fully equipped with all the facts.* 'I would like to set off immediately. I'm sure that can be arranged?'

'No doubt the King would be happy to—'

'No,' Zabrina interrupted firmly. 'I don't… I don't want the King to know about this. I need you to arrange a car to take me there, Silviana, and for the driver to be sworn to secrecy. You can tell him that I am arranging a surprise for His Majesty.' Which was true, she thought grimly. The only trouble was that she had no idea if her hunch was correct—or how it would be received if it was.

Her heart was pounding hard in her chest as she accompanied Silviana through the palace and she didn't begin to breathe normally again until she and her lady-in-waiting were driving through the streets of Rosumunte, towards the famous mountain range which dominated the capital city.

Zabrina tried to concentrate on what she was seeing but found herself not *wanting* to love the elegant trees and lush foliage as the car skimmed through the green countryside. Because what if she was exiled after all this? What if the wedding was called off because Roman was angered by her taking such a bold initiative? Could she cope with the emotional and financial fall-out of not securing a marriage deal?

She was going to have to.

Before too long, they drew up in front of an old-fashioned cottage with a thatched roof, just like the ones she'd seen in a book she'd once had, all about England. To the front there was a beautiful garden and in the distance was a goat grazing in a meadow. A young woman came running out of the house when she heard the car, her look of curiosity changing to one of shock as Zabrina stepped from the car, and hastily she sank into a deep curtsey.

'Your Royal Highness!' she gasped. 'This is indeed an unexpected honour.'

'Forgive me for this unannounced intrusion,' replied Zabrina. 'But I was wondering if I might have a word with your...grandmother? Alone, if I may.'

'Of...of course, Your Royal Highness. If you would just give me a moment to inform my *bunica* and quickly prepare the cottage.'

Zabrina could hear the murmur of voices and the clattering of china before being ushered inside the surprisingly large and very comfortable cottage, and minutes later she was sitting opposite a sprightly looking old lady in a chair which rocked before a blazing fire, despite the sunshine of the day outside.

'When you get old, you get cold,' the old lady said.

Zabrina nodded. 'I hope to have the good fortune to discover that for myself one day.' But her voice was a little choked as she spoke, her chest tight with emotion as she realised that this woman had rocked the infant Roman, had held his little hand and watched as he'd learned to walk. And then she had been summarily dismissed from his life. 'Thank you for seeing me.'

Olga's still-beautiful eyes were a little faded, but they narrowed perceptively as her gaze took in the enormous emerald and diamond engagement ring which glittered on Zabrina's finger.

'You are Roman's woman?' she asked, very softly.

This was a tricky one to answer, but how could Zabrina possibly demand the truth, if she was not prepared to speak it herself?

'I want to be.' The words came out in a rush. 'I so want to be.'

Olga folded her hands together on her lap. 'I wondered when you might come.'

Roman stared out of the window, but the sweeping beauty of the palace gardens remained nothing but a green and kaleidoscopic blur. He turned back to find Andrei regarding him with an expression of concern he hadn't seen on his aide's face in a long time. Probably not since he had masqueraded as Constantin Izvor on that fateful journey from Albastase to Petrogoria, he thought grimly.

'*Where*,' he repeated furiously, 'has she gone?'

'We don't know, Your Majesty.'

'What do you mean, you don't know? How can you not know?'

'Is the Princess not free to travel at will?' Andrei asked mildly.

Roman glared. 'Of course she is. It's just…'

Just what? Had he expected her to be pale-faced and remorseful over breakfast this morning, telling him she'd been too intrusive with her questions last night and promising him it wouldn't happen again? Yes, he had. Of course he had. For he wasn't blind to the effect he had on her—women were notoriously bad at hiding their feelings when they had begun to care deeply for a man, and he knew that cancelling their wedding was the last thing Zabrina wanted.

At first he had even been prepared to overlook her lateness, aware that she was going to have to lose face by backing down and was probably dreading making her entrance and her apology. But as his coffee had grown cold and the servants had hovered around the table anxiously, he had realised that she wasn't going to show up at all. Not only had she failed to appear, but she had neglected to do him the courtesy of informing him until much later. Wasn't such an act towards the monarch completely unacceptable?

He had gone to his offices and tried to lose himself in his work, but for once his grand schemes had failed to excite him. Even the prized Marengo Forest seemed to represent nothing but a cluster of trees which had forced him into making the most stupid decision of his life by agreeing to marry the stubborn and foxy Princess who refused to conform to his expectations of her!

Now it was getting on for midday and still she hadn't returned and his slowly ignited temper was in danger of erupting. He could hear Andrei talking quietly on his cell-phone and then the aide gently cleared his throat as he finished the call.

'Your Majesty?'

'Yes, what is it?'

'The Princess's car arrived back at the palace a short time ago and she—'

'Have her sent here as soon as she—'

'You don't have to have me *sent* anywhere,' came a voice from behind him. 'I came all of my own accord!'

He whirled around to see Zabrina standing there, a look of challenge sparking from her green eyes which matched the faint sarcasm underpinning her words. Her cheeks were flushed with roses, as if she had been outside in the fresh air, but there was no contrition on her face, he noted. No sense that she had offended him on so many levels he didn't even know where to begin.

'Where have you been?' he questioned coldly.

She opened her mouth as if to respond and then looked at Andrei.

'If you will excuse me, Your Majesty, Your Royal Highness?' said the aide smoothly, backing out of the double golden doors with indecent haste.

Roman wanted to demand that his aide stay, or that Zabrina return later, when he might deign to schedule in a slot to see her. Or even to suggest she wait until they were having lunch—because any of those propositions would demonstrate very firmly who was in charge. But the glint of determination flashing from her eyes made him realise that any such request would be futile. And besides, why not get it over with?

'So,' he said coolly, once the doors had closed behind Andrei. 'Are you going to answer my question and tell me where you've been?'

She made a big show of wiggling her shoulders so that her dark hair shimmered against the yellow blouse—the fine fabric hinting at the slender but muscular body beneath. Had she done that deliberately to emphasise her allure? he wondered achingly. To remind him how much in thrall he was to her agile physicality?

'No ideas, Roman?' she asked, with equal aplomb.

'You aren't going to accuse me of trying to seduce my new, Petrogorian groom?'

'Hardly,' he snapped. 'Since you were seen leaving by car, with Silviana!'

For a moment she looked as if she was about to smile, but then seemed to change her mind for her face took on a completely different look. Softer. Thoughtful—almost gentle. And that put the fear of God in him like nothing else, because gentleness was alien to him and he didn't trust it. Very pointedly, he lifted his arm to glance at his watch. 'Whatever it is, will you please hurry up and tell me because I haven't got all day?'

'Roman, I went to visit Olga. I found out where she lives.'

A barrage of feelings hit him. Cold fear, dark dread and anger. But anger was the overriding emotion which made him shoot out his response to her. Because wasn't it easier to focus on that, rather than confront the sudden blackness which was hovering at the edges of his mind? 'What the hell did you do that for?'

'Because I was confused by some of the things you told me.' She licked her lips. 'I guess I found it hard to believe that your mother never even wrote back to you.'

'You think all women are fundamentally good—and mothers in particular?' He gave a bitter laugh.

'In that case, I pity you your naivety, Zabrina. I lost faith in your sex a long time ago.'

But she shook her head as if he hadn't spoken. 'Some of the things you said didn't add up,' she continued. 'Why she used to hide away. Why she used to only come to you under cover of darkness. It seemed to me that Olga must have known something and she did. That was another reason why she was sacked.'

Roman's heart clenched as if some malevolent iron fist were squeezing it tighter and tighter. He wanted to turn and run, or to put his hands to his ears like a child and block out whatever was coming. But that would be the behaviour of a coward, and he was no coward. And hadn't he weathered the worst of the storm all those years ago? What could possibly be left to hurt him now? 'What did Olga know?'

She sucked in a deep breath and now he saw the flicker of fear and darkness in her own eyes. 'Your father used to abuse your mother,' she said. 'Mentally and physically.'

'No!' The word thundered from his lungs. 'That is not possible.'

'Why not?'

'Because I would have known.' He could hear the break in his voice as he shook his head in denial. 'I would have protected her.'

'No, Roman. You would not have known, because your mother wouldn't have wanted you to know. She wanted to hide her pain and distress from you. She wanted to protect *you*, which is a mother's instinct. And how could a small boy possibly save a woman from the wrath of his powerful and autocratic father? That would only have put you in danger and that was the last thing she would have wanted.'

He curled his fingers into his palms so hard that he could feel the deep imprint of his nails, but the sharpness of that didn't come close to the fierce stabbing of his heart. 'How could you possibly know what she wanted?' he raged. 'Are you the one who is now capable of reading minds?'

'No. But I have helped many women like your mother at my refuge in Albastase—'

'Poor women?' he demanded in disbelief.

'Yes, poor women—and some rich ones, too. As well as all the others in between. Because abuse knows no age or class boundaries, Roman, and there are victims everywhere. Olga told me that your mother often used to have black eyes. That was why she would read your bedtime story in darkness and why she sometimes ducked out of sight if she saw you walking down the corridor. It was why she had to leave, because she knew she was incapable of being a good and loving mother towards you, if she was constantly being beaten down.'

'Then why…why didn't she take me with her?'

Zabrina heard the raw note of anguish in his voice as he whispered out that stark and heartbreaking question and she wanted so much to comfort him.

To take him in her arms and hold him. But not now. Not yet. Because didn't he need to *feel* this? To *really* feel it—to have the ugly wound laid wide open after all these years, so he would be able to recover from it at last? Afterwards—maybe once he'd heard the whole story—that would be the time to offer him solace. If he still wanted her. 'She tried to take you,' she said simply. 'But, of course, your father discovered her plans and made sure she was spirited away in his private jet in the dead of night, while you were fast asleep. I don't know if you can imagine how different those times were, but a waitress from Missouri would have had no clout against one of the most powerful men in the world.'

'She never got my letters?' he questioned suddenly.

Zabrina bit her lip, because, oh, how she wished she could sugar-coat this one. But she couldn't do that either. 'I don't think so. I suspect the letters might have been destroyed as soon as you dispatched them,' she said. 'But she wrote to *you*.'

He narrowed his eyes and the flare of hope he was so desperately trying to repress made her heart turn over with love and sorrow.

'She wrote to you through Olga, but the letters only got through after your father died. I have them.'

There was a long silence while Roman digested this and he could feel the powerful thunder of his heart as he looked at the Princess who stood before him, her green eyes wide with compassion. 'Why did I never receive them?' he demanded, but deep in his heart he knew the reason.

'Olga tried to contact you after your father's death,' she said gently. 'But she was blocked every time. By you.'

He nodded, painfully aware of his own contribution to what had happened. 'Because the thought of seeing and speaking to her again after all those years was more than I could endure,' he said slowly, almost as if he had forgotten she was in the room with him. Was that why he did nothing to conceal the bitter break in his voice? Or because he knew that his Princess would understand? 'I couldn't bear the thought of reliving…' He swallowed. 'Of reliving all that pain.'

'I realise that,' Zabrina whispered. 'And so does she. She knows you were responsible for the anonymous donations paid into her bank account for so many years and she thanks you for your generosity.'

'I want to hate my father for what he did,' he said, his voice changing into a rasp. 'In fact, I *do* hate him.'

'Well, don't,' she whispered. 'Just let it go, Roman. For hate brings nothing of value to anyone's life and you don't know the truth about his own upbringing, I assume?'

He shook his head. 'No. No, I don't. He never wanted to discuss it. He never wanted to discuss anything.' His father had never *talked* to him, not properly. It had been like living with an automaton who had demanded increasingly high levels of perfection from his only child. Had he ever felt guilty about the way he'd treated the woman he had married? Could that have been the cause of the unexpected tears he had shed, just before shuddering out his final breath, his hand tightly clutching that of his son? Roman gave a heavy sigh because Zabrina was right. He needed to forgive, or there would be no peace in his own heart. His thoughts cleared and he looked into her clear, bright gaze, his mouth feeling as if it had been crammed full of stones as he asked the question he had been dreading.

'And my mother?' he asked, bracing himself for the inevitable reply.

'She's alive,' Zabrina said, very quietly.

He froze. 'Are you serious?'

She nodded. 'Totally serious. Your mother is alive and well, Roman. She sent you this.'

She bent and reached into her handbag and pulled out a small pouch and inside was a delicate necklace—a cheap silver chain with a blue enamel bird dangling from the end. 'It's a bluebird,' she whispered, as she let it spill into his open palm. 'The symbol of Missouri state, where she comes from. She sent it to Olga, with one of her first letters. She wants to see you. We could invite her to the wedding, if you like. Or you could go and see her on your own, if…if you don't want the wedding to go ahead.'

His fingers closed around the little locket. 'You're saying you want to call it off?' he husked.

Zabrina closed her eyes in despair as she watched him replace the necklace in the pouch and put it in his pocket. How could he be so *dense*? How could he fail to see the evidence which was before his eyes, that she wanted him so much she would walk to the ends of the earth for him? But deep down she knew the answer to that. Because he hadn't been shown enough love in his life—that was why he couldn't recognise it. His trust in love had been destroyed and this was her chance to help him rebuild it, and she had to take it, no matter what the outcome. Even if he felt she now knew too much about him, to be comfortable with them sharing a life.

'Calling it off is the last thing I want to do,' she said. 'I want to be your wife more than anything in the world, because I love you, Roman. I think I've loved you from the first time I saw you, when you were Constantin Izvor. I loved you as the man, not as the King, but I love the King too—if that makes sense. You make me laugh and you bring me joy, and, yes, you can be infuriating at times but I'm sure I can, too.'

'Zabrina—'

'No. Let me finish, because this bit is important,' she said in a low voice which, infuriatingly, had started shaking. 'When I told you all those things about what I expected from our marriage, I was wrong. When I said I would turn a blind eye if you wanted to have affairs with other women, I don't know what I was thinking. Well, I do actually, but I wasn't being honest with myself. Because the truth is that I would be beside myself with jealousy and rage if you ever touched another woman. I want you exclusively, Roman, maybe even a bit possessively. So if that isn't your idea of what you want out of a royal marriage, then—'

'Zabrina, Zabrina, Zabrina.' He pulled her into his arms and smoothed his thumb down the side of her face as if he were seeing it for the first time. 'I never wanted that kind of marriage and the thought of you being with anyone other than me repels me. In fact, the idea of you being jealous is rather reassuring— because we both know that I'm capable of feeling it, too.' He paused and his voice was a little unsteady. 'Except that I will never give you cause to be jealous, because I love you, Princess.'

'You don't have to say that,' she whispered.

'I know I don't. I'm not in the habit of saying anything I don't mean and I don't intend to start now. But learning how to express myself is a whole new skill set, so you will have to make allowances for me.'

She smiled. 'Oh, I think I could manage to do that, my darling.'

She touched her fingers to his jaw and Roman could see the wonder shining from her face and her sweet expression smote at a heart which was already full and somehow all the pain was just draining away from him, leaving him feeling as if he'd shed a heavy burden he hadn't even realised he'd been carrying. It would have been so easy to kiss her and allow their bodies to help heal the pain and take away the sense of time wasted, and a mother's love denied. But this was too important to take the easy way out. He needed to find the right words to say to her and make sure she believed them. 'Just like you,' he said slowly, 'I fell in love the first time we met and wished you weren't a princess so I could just go ahead and seduce you.'

'But you seduced me anyway!'

'So I did.' He sighed. 'I don't know if you can appreciate just how out of character that was for me, Zabrina—to shrug off my sense of duty and make as if it didn't matter. And I resented you for that. I resented your power over me.'

'You never wanted a woman to have that perceived power over you again,' she guessed slowly. 'Because you didn't want to risk being hurt again. I understand that. But I will never hurt you, Roman—certainly not intentionally—and if I do, then you must tell me and we'll talk about it.'

He felt his heart lurch. 'I want to marry you,' he breathed. 'If I could marry you here and now, then I would. And because these words do not feature in the official Petrogorian ceremony I will say them to you now. You are the most beautiful woman I've ever met—both inside and out. You are brave and strong and caring and I am blessed to have you in my life. I love you with every fibre of my being, Zabrina. Believe me when I tell you that.'

'Oh, I do,' she whispered, the break of emotion in her voice fracturing her response. 'I so do.'

EPILOGUE

'Oh, Zabrina, you look so beautiful.' Eva clapped her hands over her mouth as she stared up at her big sister. 'Like a real queen!'

'That's because,' said Daria, glancing at the diamond-encrusted watch which had been a bridesmaid gift from her future brother-in-law, 'in approximately an hour's time she will *be* a queen! Are you nervous, Zabrina?'

Zabrina shook her head so that her tulle veil shimmered. 'Not nervous,' she said softly. 'Just happy.' She sighed. So very happy. Because Roman made her happy every second of every day. Soon she would legally be his wife and she couldn't wait. She wanted to start on this new phase of life with him. The two of them, together, as man and wife. She heard the sound of distant trumpets playing a triumphant Petrogorian fanfare and, turning to both her sisters, she gave a smile so wide it felt as if it might split her face in two. 'Shall we go?'

As they nodded, she reached out and took the fra-

grant white bouquet from Silviana, the gilded doors
were flung open and she began to make her way
down the aisle towards her beloved King. Embroidered with over one thousand tiny pearls, the train
of her dress was heavy, which meant she had to walk
slowly. But she *wanted* to walk slowly. She wanted to
make the most of every second of her wedding day
to her one true love. To the powerful soulmate who
had emerged from all the turmoil and heartbreak as
a different man, once all the barriers with which he'd
surrounded himself had come tumbling down. She
could see him standing waiting for her beneath an
arch of flowers, his pewter eyes dark, a gleam of anticipation in their depths as he watched her approach.

Faces turned as she walked—some she recognised but many she didn't. Her parents were there,
of course. Her mother sitting bolt upright in her recently cleaned 'best' crown and her father paying
rather too much attention to the busty redhead seated
at the end of the row. Zabrina found herself wondering how they would adapt to being grandparents.
Maybe a brand-new generation would bring a little
light and freshness into their cynical relationship.
You could but hope.

Along the aisle she moved, watching heads in-
cline and women curtsey. There were members of
the Albastasian aristocracy alongside their Petrogorian counterparts—as well as royals from Maraban,
from Greece and from Britain. There were A-list actors and academics—and a devastatingly handsome

but rather dangerous-looking Sheikh called Zulfaqar, whom Daria had been flirting with all during the rehearsal last night. Zabrina intended have a stern word with her sister after the ceremony and warn her off, because apparently the desert King had a terrible reputation with women. But for now, she just wanted to reach her beloved Roman and say her vows.

Her heart was beating very fast as she handed her bouquet to Daria, and as she saw Olga sitting in the front row, with three of her grandchildren, Zabrina felt a great tremble of emotion. Maybe she *was* more nervous than she'd thought. But the moment Roman grasped her fingers within the warmth of his, she felt nothing but a powerful sense of excitement and contentment filling her heart.

'You look beautiful,' he murmured.

She could feel her cheeks grow warm. 'Beautiful for you.'

His eyes narrowed as he looked down at her and she realised that he wasn't seeing the spectacular white gown, or the white tulle veil held in place by a glittering diamond crown. Instead, his gaze was fixed on the chain which hung from her neck. A cheap little silver chain from which dangled a tiny bluebird. Her 'something blue', worn by every traditional bride.

Roman's mother hadn't come to the wedding. During a very exciting video call, she had explained that it was *their* day and she didn't want to take any attention away from that. But they were planning to

visit Missouri during their honeymoon and Zabrina's
brother was very jealous because Kansas City was
the setting of one of his favourite films. And Roman
was still getting his head around the fact that he had
three half-brothers!

He had also invited her three siblings to stay during the long vacation and said he intended to do this
every year if they were keen—and to instruct Alex
in the art of kingship at the same time. He was also
quietly intending to put a diamond mine in trust,
so that her brother should have no financial woes,
should he ever inherit a large national debt.

And when Roman had revealed that the priceless
emerald and diamond necklace she'd worn on the
night of the ball—and which she *hated*—had been
a placatory gift intended to make amends for his deception on the train, Zabrina had wasted no time in
chiding him. But not for very long. She had asked
if she might sell it and use the funds raised to open
a women's refuge in Rosumunte and Roman had
agreed. As she had observed, the world was going
through a bit of a crisis at the moment and people like
her needed to lead by example. Because she didn't
need *things*. The only thing she needed was him.

He lifted her fingers to his lips and as the trumpets gave their final flourish, he spoke against her
skin, but so softly that only she could hear.

'You bring me utter joy, Zabrina. Do you know that?'

'Sssh,' she said. 'The congregation will be reading your lips.'

'I don't care—let them read to their heart's content. I need to say this and I need to say it now. I think you know how much I love you, my Princess. Just as I think you know I always will.'

Blinking back tears, she nodded, trying to compose herself in preparation for the sacred vows she would shortly make. Later, she would bring him even more joy when she told him about the baby growing beneath her breast. A baby they hadn't planned quite so soon, but something told her Roman was going to be a wonderful father.

She wanted to laugh and she wanted to cry. She was caught in the crossfire of so many powerful and conflicting emotions that suddenly she didn't care about lip-readers either.

'I love you too, my darling Roman,' she whispered. 'I love you so very much.'

And a single tear of happiness rolled all the way down her cheek and dripped onto the tiny enamel bluebird.

* * * * *

Wrapped up in
One Night Before the Royal Wedding?
*You're sure to love these other stories
by Sharon Kendrick!*

The Argentinian's Baby of Scandal
His Contract Christmas Bride
Cinderella in the Sicilian's World
The Sheikh's Royal Announcement
Cinderella's Christmas Secret

All available now

WE HOPE YOU ENJOYED
THIS BOOK FROM
⟨H⟩HARLEQUIN

PRESENTS

Escape to exotic locations where passion knows no bounds.

Welcome to the glamorous lives of royals and billionaires, where passion knows no bounds. Be swept into a world of luxury, wealth and exotic locations.

8 NEW BOOKS AVAILABLE EVERY MONTH!

HPHALO2021

#3901 BRIDE BEHIND THE DESERT VEIL
The Marchetti Dynasty
by Abby Green
After surrendering to passion with a mystery woman, Sharif Marchetti must erase their desert encounter from his memory. Until they meet again...as he lifts the veil of his convenient wife!

#3902 THE ITALIAN'S FORBIDDEN VIRGIN
Those Notorious Romanos
by Carol Marinelli
Italian tycoon Gian de Luca knows Ariana Romano is off-limits. She's his mentor's daughter, and her drama queen reputation precedes her. But when he offers her comfort one night, he's shocked to discover she's a virgin. Perhaps he's been wrong about her all along...

#3903 HIS STOLEN INNOCENT'S VOW
The Queen's Guard
by Marcella Bell
For billionaire Drake Andros, only marriage and an heir from Helene d'Tierrza will recover what was stolen from him. Their chemistry may persuade her to help him, but her vow of innocence may complicate his plan...

#3904 ONE HOT NEW YORK NIGHT
Wanted: A Billionaire
by Melanie Milburne
A sizzling night of passion is exactly what Zoey Brackenfield needs. And since it's with Finn O'Connell, business rival and notorious playboy, there's zero chance of heartbreak. That is, until she starts craving his exhilarating touch...

For billionaire Drake Andros, only marriage and an heir from Helene d'Tierrza will recover what was stolen from him. Their chemistry may persuade her to help him, but her vow of innocence may complicate his plan...

Read on for a sneak preview of Marcella Bell's next story for Harlequin Presents
His Stolen Innocent's Vow.

"I can't," she repeated, her voice low and earnest. "I can't, because when I went to him as he lay dying, I looked him in his eyes and swore to him that the d'Tierrza line would end with me, that there would be no d'Tierrza children to inherit the lands or title and that I would see to it that the family name was wiped from the face of the earth so that everything he had ever worked for, or cared about, was lost to history, the legacy he cared so much about nothing but dust. I swore to him that I would never marry and never have children, that not a trace of his legacy would be left on this planet."

For a moment, there was a pause, as if the room itself had sucked in a hiss of irritation. The muscles in his neck tensed, then flexed, though he remained otherwise motionless. He blinked as if in slow motion, the movement a sigh, carrying something much deeper than frustration, though no sound came out. Hel's chest squeezed as she merely observed him. She felt like she'd let him down in some monumental way, though they'd only just become reacquainted. She struggled to understand why the sensation was so familiar until she recognized the experience of being in the presence of her father.

Then he opened his eyes again, and instead of the cold green disdain her heart expected, they still burned that fascinating warm brown—a heat that was a steady home fire, as comforting as the imaginary family she'd dreamed up as a child—and all of the taut disappointment in the air was gone.

Her vow was a hiccup in his plans. That he had a low tolerance for hiccups was becoming clear. How she knew any of this when he had revealed so little in his reaction, and her mind only now offered up hazy memories of him as a young man, she didn't know.

She offered a shrug and an airy laugh in consolation, mildly embarrassed about the whole thing though she was simultaneously unsure as to exactly why. "Otherwise, you know, I'd be all in. Despite the whole abduction…" Her cheeks were hot, likely bright pink, but it couldn't be helped, so she made the joke anyway, despite the risk that it might bring his eyes to her face, that it might mean their gazes locked again and he stole her breath again.

Of course, that was what happened. And then there was that smile again, the one that said he knew all about the strange, mesmerizing power he had over her, and it pleased him.

Whether he was the kind of man who used his power for good or evil had yet to be determined.

Either way, beneath that infuriating smile, deep in his endless brown eyes, was the sharp attunement of a predator locked on its target. "Give me a week." His face may not have changed, but his voice gave him away, a trace of hoarseness, as if his sails had been slashed and the wind slipped through them, threaded it, a strange hint of something Hel might have described as desperation…if it had come from anyone other than him.

"What?" she asked.

"Give me a week to change your mind."

Don't miss
His Stolen Innocent's Vow.
Available April 2021 wherever
Harlequin Presents books and ebooks are sold.

Harlequin.com

Love Harlequin romance?

DISCOVER.

Be the first to find out about promotions,
news and exclusive content!

 Facebook.com/HarlequinBooks

 Twitter.com/HarlequinBooks

 Instagram.com/HarlequinBooks

 Pinterest.com/HarlequinBooks

 YouTube.com/HarlequinBooks

ReaderService.com

EXPLORE.

Sign up for the Harlequin e-newsletter and
download a free book from any series at
TryHarlequin.com

CONNECT.

Join our Harlequin community to
share your thoughts and connect
with other romance readers!
Facebook.com/groups/HarlequinConnection

HARLEQUIN

HSOCIAL2021